Rescuing You for Christmas

A LOVE IN LEAVENWORTH, WA NOVELLA

JUDY LESLIE

ISBN: 979-8-9857784-7-2

Ebook: 979-8-9857784-8-9

Cover Design by Covered by Melinda

www.coveredbyMelinda.com

To my daughter Paige

And for everyone that believes in the magic of Christmas!

A Love in Leavenworth Christmas Novella

By Judy Leslie

Also by Judy Leslie

Love in Leavenworth Series

Renovating Hearts

Heart Strings

Love Among the Flames

Hearts Uncorked

Cook's Cove Mystery, Romance Series

The House at The Cove

No Place to Hide

Desperate Strokes

Taken From The Sea

Shadows from the Past

To learn about bargains and upcoming books go to Judy's website at
www.judy-leslie.com

* * *

Rescuing You
for
Christmas

Contents

Chapter One

PAIGE

Trembling, I grip the steering wheel tightly. The windshield wipers are flying back and forth. Snow is coming down hard, making it impossible to see more than a few feet in front of my car. My heart races with every slight movement as my tires slip on the icy road.

From the back seat, I hear my daughter Sarah's voice, tinged with worry. She's five years old and clutching her teddy next to her chest. "Are we going to be okay, Mommy?"

"Yes, there's only a little ice," I reply, trying to sound calm. "Just hold on tight, sweetie."

As I follow the winding mountain highway, I focus on where the road is. I've driven in snow before, but never in conditions like this. The car's headlights barely penetrate the swirling snowflakes.

As we round another bend, the rear lights of the car in front of me disappear. I worry that I'll lose the only clue to where the road is.

Suddenly, there is a loud thud, and the car jerks forward. My heart skips a beat as I fight to keep control of the vehicle, but it's useless. The car is spinning out of control, careening off the side of the road. I hear a small cry from the backseat as we jolt into a snowbank and come to an abrupt stop. A blanket of powdery snow covers the windshield.

My heart is pounding as I frantically turn to check on Sarah, who is wide-eyed.

"How do you feel, sweetie?"

"I'm fine." Her voice is shaky.

I let out the breath I was holding. Thank God she isn't hurt.

"Are you okay, Mommy?" she asks, her voice shaking.

"Yes, honey," I take a deep breath. I'm still trembling from the ordeal.

"Are we stuck in the snow?"

I have no idea what to expect outside, but I say, "I'll go and check." I bite my lip, then unbuckle my seatbelt. Fumbling a bit, I push against the door, and it opens. The ground is deep slush, and I reluctantly place one foot outside and then the next. My feet skid out from underneath me as I stand up, sending me down into the mush. Now I'm sitting in the freezing, wet snow. I glance around, hoping to find someone in another car nearby, but whoever or whatever hit me is long gone.

"Swell," I mutter as I try to figure out how I'm going to get up. Each attempt is worthless. The four-inch heels of my boots are too unsteady to stand on in this slippery muck. My hands are freezing. I stare up at the door handle. If I can only reach it, I can pull myself up. "Help," I whisper to myself in the silence.

The snow is letting up a little. I hear a car go by. Then another. I am going to have to figure out something before I freeze to death out here. I turn and crawl onto my knees.

There's the crunch of snow from a few feet away—a car

rolling to a stop behind me. Then, I make out a dark shape heading in my direction through the swirling flakes.

"Thank God," I mutter.

"Are you okay?" a man calls. His voice is deep, and his breath frosts into the air as he peers around the side of the car.

I'm not okay. I'm stuck in freezing slush, being pelted by white flakes. "Over here," I yell.

I look up to see a tall man in a dark knitted hat and a blue ski parka reaching out his hand to help me. I grab it and try standing, but my foot slides, and one heel breaks off with a sharp snap. *Damn, these were expensive shoes.*

I stagger and almost fall on my butt again, but the man wraps his arms around my waist, lifting me to my feet. I glance up—and then farther up—at his bearded face. He must be six-two at least, and he's looking down at me, his eyes a sharp and dazzling blue. When he releases me to stand on my own, I feel like a stork with one foot in a pond of ice as I lean against the open door to my car.

He huffs out a breath as his eyes scan my car. The wheels twisted nearly sideways. "Looks to me like you're going to need a tow to get your car out."

"Great," I mutter. I can't help but look back at the man who'd come to my rescue. To match his jacket, he's wearing blue and black waterproof pants and heavy boots. It looks as though he's just come from a day of skiing.

"Were you going far? I can give you a lift."

I hesitate. He seems friendly enough, but you never know these days. But he's smiling at me, and the corners of his eyes crinkle in a friendly and attractive way. I'm not one to jump to trusting strange men out of the blue, but there is something about him that seems familiar. Or comforting, perhaps. He seems to be the very definition of small-town friendliness. What the heck? Maybe he can help me out.

"I don't suppose you'd be willing to drive us back to Seattle?" My tone is wistful. I'd planned a grand Christmas adventure, but my breaking point for adventure had come about five minutes ago when we'd slid off the edge of the road.

"I'm afraid they've closed the road in that direction." He rubs a hand through his beard, which has ice crystals forming from his breath. "Your only way out of here is east."

"Oh." I can't help the disappointed tone in my voice, and I know he hears it. I peer through the glass of the back window, which is fogged. Sarah isn't paying attention to us—she seems to be talking to her teddy. I straighten up. "We were on our way to a cabin I rented in Leavenworth to stay for Christmas."

"Well, that I can do," he says. "I was headed in that direction anyway."

I hesitate, but then say, "Thanks." I'm not thrilled with the idea of accepting a ride from a stranger. But what else can I do? Taking my phone out of my pocket, it doesn't appear to work. My heart sinks a little. Even so, I let my fingers fly over the keys and typed in a message to my best friend.

> Car stuck in snow near Christmas cabin.
> Cute stranger offered me a ride. If I'm
> murdered, send help!

I hit "send" and get the notification that the message will go out when my phone has service.

I pocket my cell and say, "No reception." The man nods as I glance at the nose of my car stuck in the snow. "I hope there isn't too much damage. I'm going to need to drive back home after Christmas."

"I'll call once we get cell coverage and ask that they tow your car to Leavenworth for repairs."

I bite my lip. "Do you have any idea how long that's going to take?"

"I don't know. It will depend on how much damage you sustained and how many other vehicles they have to fix. Also, if they need to send off for parts."

"Do you know if I get a rental car somewhere?"

He shakes his head. "We can try calling around, but I doubt it. Most places would be booked out for the holidays."

I almost groan. "So, I'm going to be stuck at the cabin until it's fixed with no form of transportation?"

"Looks that way."

I blow out a long breath that turns into a poof of air. "It's a good thing I've brought enough food for our stay." I begin to shake from shock and the chill. With my teeth chattering, I say, "I've booked the cabin for a couple of weeks, but we should have enough."

"That's good. Hang on, you're in no state to stay outside. Let's get you to my car, and I'll grab your stuff."

Sarah knocks on the glass. The child safety lock prevents her from opening the back door, but she sticks her head around the front seat and calls out, "Mommy, I'm cold."

She has her pink blanket wrapped around her. Without a jacket, I'm sure she's feeling the chill. I know I'm freezing, and I have my wool coat on.

The man puts one palm on the roof of the car and leans down to smile inside at Sarah.

"Hello, there." He gets a shy wave in return, and then he straightens back up to face me. "I didn't know you had a little one with you. We better get her inside so she can warm up."

I open the back door and lift Sarah up, wrapping my coat

around her to keep her warm. "This nice man has offered to drive us to our cabin."

I glance at him, and he seems to understand—my shoes aren't suited for carrying a little girl through the snow. He nods at me.

"He's going to carry you over to his car so you don't fall."

"My name is Matt Holloway, by the way." He grins. Whether the expression is directed at me or my daughter, I can't tell. But it transforms his face completely. Before, he was handsome in a rugged, mountain man kind of way. That smile, though—it transforms him into GQ material.

I realize I've been staring at him for a few seconds when he clears his throat to prompt me. I stammer, "Pai-Paige Anderson. And this is my daughter, Sarah."

"Hi, Sarah." Matt reaches out his arms, and I reluctantly let my daughter go as he scoops her up against his chest. He starts to head to his truck, then turns back to me.

"Why don't you sit in your car so you don't fall again?"

I mentally measure the distance from my car to his, but I know there's no way I can make it, even if the heel of my boot wasn't broken. Matt also doesn't look like the child-stealing type. The snow is still coming down heavily, so I just have to trust him. I watch him walk away, open his car door, and deposit her inside. His car is running, and I'm guessing that the heat must be on.

I undo Sarah's car seat and hand it to him. He carries it to his car and then installs in his back seat, then buckles up my daughter in it. I'm relieved to see him come back for me.

When he reaches me, I grab his arm and try to navigate over the slippery snow. After my legs nearly go out from under me, he wraps one arm around my waist to support me. It's been so many years since a man has held me, and I resist the instinctual urge to push away. I really can't walk with my boots and the snow, and his arm is solid and comforting. We reach his truck together, and Matt opens the door and lifts me into the front seat of his SUV. "Hold tight," he says, and then goes back for Sarah's booster seat and my luggage.

After three trips, I hear his voice from the back. "You didn't tell me you were moving in. How many boxes did you bring?" His tone is gruff and a little bit annoyed.

I guess I would be, too. I smile sheepishly back at him, but he doesn't seem to notice as he pushes forward one of the boxes to make room for the rest.

"I brought decorations for the tree, and ingredients for Christmas cookies."

"Hm. Good thing I've got room for all this stuff," he replies.

After a few more trips back and forth in the snow, he clambers into the driver's seat, shakes the white flakes off his hat, and we are on our way.

Matt looks in both directions before pulling out onto the icy road. His large, capable-looking hands grip the steering wheel lightly but firmly, and he carefully navigates the slippery roads with confidence.

Sarah seems to have gotten over her shyness. She's never met a stranger that she didn't consider a friend. She sits behind us, chattering with excitement about spending time at the cabin. It's endearing, and despite the accident and the inconvenience of relying on a stranger, I'm suddenly glad again that I've planned this special trip. Matt seems entertained with my daughter's babbling about Santa's reindeer.

"Maybe, once your mom's car is fixed, you two can visit the reindeer farm in Leavenworth.

"Really?" I think Sarah's voice will go through the roof. "Is that where Santa keeps his Rudolph?"

Matt laughs. "I don't know. But if he does, I bet it's a secret."

I listen in, grateful for the distraction. Matt seems like a kind and genuine person who likes kids. His tone is easy, and he doesn't seem to be bothered by my daughter's chatter at all. I take a moment to study his profile. He must feel my gaze because he looks over at me. His blue eyes twinkle when he gives me a slow smile. I give him a quick smile back, but glance down at my hands before the moment can get awkward. However, I can't help but notice him looking at me several more times during the trip. He seems just as curious about me as I am about him. I give him the address so he knows where to drop us off.

As he drives deeper into the woods, the snow lets up for the moment, showing off a winter wonderland around us with all the trees draped in white. It reminds me of a Christmas card—almost too perfect to be real. Sarah's excitement only grows as we see a cabin in the distance. Matt points it out as our destination.

Only a few more moments, and then Matt pulls to a stop. As he opens his door and gets out, I crawl over the seat to the back of his SUV, quickly rummaging through my luggage for the matching pair of yellow rubber boots I'd packed for Sarah and me. My eight-hundred-dollar leather pair of stiletto heels are now officially trashed. No doubt my designer wool coat has a water stain on the back of it, too. At least the knees to my pants have dried out on the way here.

A frigid blast of wind greets me when I step out of the car and turn to face our holiday vacation rental. But when I look at it, my heart sinks. The cabin is nothing like the pictures I saw on the website. Its walls of wooden shingles, which looked so picturesque and Christmassy in the posted photos, have missing slats in places, giving it a patchwork appearance. Half the shutters on the windows are missing, one at the front hanging down to the ground and supported by a lone nail. To top it all off, the pathway leading to the front door has knee-high snow, as if it hasn't been shoveled since the start of winter. Everything looks old and in terrible disrepair.

This is the place we'll be stuck in for the next two weeks? Jeez.

A voice behind me echoes my dismal thoughts. "You've got to be kidding me. You rented this place?" Matt shakes his head. "Are you sure you want to stay here?"

First the car wreck, now this. My eyes sting, and I feel like crying. Instead, I reply with a short, "Yes." I wipe the snow from my eyelashes, ignoring the moisture. "It's probably better inside." At least, I hope so. My voice sounds fake even to my own ears, but I'm trying to keep my spirits up.

Matt seems to understand I need a moment because he opens the back of the SUV and takes out a shovel. His voice is soft and comforting when he says, "I'll clear the snow off the walkway for you."

His offer gets me motivated to shake off the disappointment I'm feeling. Things could definitely be way worse. Even though I had my doubts when Matt first pulled up to rescue us, he's turned out to be solid and dependable. The least I owe him is to keep it together. "Do you have another shovel? I can help."

Matt scans me up and down, lingering on my bright yellow boots. If I didn't feel so depressed about how our holiday trip was turning out, I might have minded his amused look.

"I doubt it," he says, smiling. He shakes his head. "It's okay. Get back in the car and crank up the heat."

Gratefully, I retreat to the warmth of the SUV. I watch as Matt throws scoopfuls of snow to the side, his breath visible in the cold air. I appreciate his effort, which makes me feel better about the situation.

After Matt clears a path, the three of us make our way to the front door. Sarah hovers next to me while I fumble with the lock and struggle to open it. Inside, after flipping the switch on and off several times, it becomes apparent that the electricity is not working.

I peer into the darkness. "Just great," I mutter, more and more frustrated by the minute. It's better to be irritated than fall apart, I guess. At least it's keeping me warm.

"I'll get a flashlight and check the fuse box."

I feel a small, cold hand closing around my index finger and grip it for all she's worth. Matt returns with two flashlights and hands me one.

I shine the light around. The interior of the cabin is just as bad as the outside. The furniture sags in the middle of each seat, the walls covered in mysterious smudges that are reminiscent of a horror movie, and there is a musty and unpleasant smell permeating from every corner of the room.

Sarah looks up at me with tears in her eyes. "Mommy, I don't like it here. I want to go home."

A pang of guilt fills my chest. She's been through so much on this trip. This is not what I had in mind when I promised Sarah a special Christmas this year.

Matt returns with more bad news. "It looks like someone shut off the power to the house." Matt rubs the back of his neck. "You can't stay here."

He pulls out his phone and puts it on speaker as he hits speed dial. It rings once before a pleasant voice says hello.

"Hey, Amber. Any chance you have room for a woman and her daughter? They're stranded here while their car gets fixed."

Amber's voice bounces back against the dark and dismal room. "Sorry, Matt. You know how it is this time of year. Linda and Don are staying with me until New Year's. Did you try calling Mom?"

"Her place is booked, so I didn't bother."

"Chris doesn't have any room either, and Grady and Kim have guests too."

"That's what I figured. Thanks, anyway." Matt ends the call and turns to me. His blue eyes are sympathetic. "Sorry, my last resorts are full. This is the worst time of year to be looking for a place to stay." He hesitates and runs his fingers down his beard. "The best I can offer you is to stay at my house for now."

"Your house? Won't your wife object?"

"I live alone." He shrugs. "If the weather was better, I'd offer to drive you the forty miles to the next town. But the snow's only getting worse. I hate to say it, but it looks like that's your only choice for now."

I slump my shoulders. "Really?"

"Come on, let's go before your daughter gets a chill."

I follow Matt's footsteps in the snow, holding onto Sarah's hand tightly. We pile back into the car and head back down the road.

The only sound is the swishing of an occasional passing car and the windshield wipers as we drive. Before we've gone for three minutes, Sarah is conked out in the backseat.

After seeing the place I rented, I'm completely depressed. It's almost as if I ate some un-Lucky Charms for breakfast today before we set out from Seattle. I spent a month organizing our Christmas plans, and now they're ruined.

In that small part of me that's not wallowing in misery, I'm aware that it's nice of Matt to offer us a place to stay. But I don't know him at all. The thought of staying with a stranger for the holidays makes me extremely uncomfortable. Especially a tall, dark drink of water like him.

Well, I guess I'm going to have to deal with it for now and make the best of the situation. Perhaps a cancelation will open up space at one of the town's inns after this snowstorm.

I glance over my shoulder. Luckily, Sarah's snuggled with a blanket and completely oblivious to my concerns.

When we arrive at Matt's cabin, I hesitate before getting out of the car. I can't help but feel guilty—and a bit awkward—for imposing on him.

"Hey, are you okay?" he asks. His voice is laced with concern, and it sounds completely genuine.

I look down. "Yeah, I'm fine. Of course, I'm questioning my life choices right about now..." I glance up again and force a smile, "but thank you."

His eyes are penetrating for a second, but then he seems to take me at face value. "Okay. Let me get Sarah for you. I don't want you to slip while carrying her." He unfastens Sarah's seatbelt and gently picks her up, carefully keeping her nestled under her blanket. He holds her against his chest while he unlocks the front door and brings her inside.

I follow the two of them in and glance around. The walls are made of logs, and the wooden floors creak softly under our feet. The main room of the cabin is spacious, with a high ceiling supported by wooden beams. The word "rustic" immediately springs to mind. A set of overstuffed armchairs and a well-worn sofa sits in front of a stone fireplace. The kitchen opens onto the room in an open-air floor plan, with what looks like a handmade wooden dining table and four matching chairs dividing the space. It isn't fancy, but it is certainly miles better than the cabin I rented.

Matt lays Sarah on the couch, her thin, pink blanket wrapped around her. He goes down the hallway and returns with a thick plaid blanket that he places gently on top of her. In her sleep, she turns her face and snuggles deeper beneath the warmth.

He turns to me, but can't quite seem to meet my eyes. I'm having the same trouble. With Sarah asleep, the intimacy of being face-to-face and planning to cohabit strikes a bit too close to home.

"This place is small, and I rarely have house guests, so we'll have to figure out how to avoid stepping on each other's toes while you're here," Matt mumbles.

Hunh. So, I guess he's not as "Mr. Nice Guy" as I thought. I cross my arms over my chest and seem to have no problems meeting his eyes after all. My tone is dry when I reply, "I'm not really thrilled by the idea of being at a stranger's mercy either."

Matt seems to dip his head. "I'm sorry," he says. "That was really rude of me to say out loud." He jangles his keys in his hand before turning to the door. "I'll get your stuff from my car and be right back."

While Matt is gone, I peek around his house.

First stop is the kitchen. It's tucked into a corner of the main room, with a large, black, cast-iron stove against one wall. Before visions of washing laundry in a stream and outhouses start to terrify me, I'm relieved to see a regular electric stove, too. I wasn't sure how rustic this place was going to be, but it seems we're not going to go full Paul Bunyan, thank goodness.

There's a deep sink with a wooden drying rack filled with

colorful, mismatched dishes. A Crock-Pot is on, and I sniff at the air. Something smells delicious. There's the savory odor of bubbling beef and caramelized onions—stew, I guess. Over the sink is a window that looks out onto the snow-covered trees in the yard.

I go down the hall and discover two small bedrooms through two open doorways. A collection of books sit stacked neatly on a small wooden shelf in one bedroom, which I assume to be Matt's. I next look to the guest room across the hall. Before I can check on the third room to see what is behind the only closed door, I hear the stomp of footsteps approaching the front door. Spinning around, I dash back to the living room so I won't be caught snooping.

The door is pulled open, and a stack of boxes—followed by Matt carefully navigating his way—come inside with a swirl of snow and cold. As soon as Matt sets the boxes inside, I point out which ones are supposed to go to the kitchen. He carries two of them, and I grab the third, and together we place them on the counter.

"What's all this other stuff?" he asks, gesturing toward the plastic bins in the entry.

"I brought some Christmas decorations," I reply. After I say it, I glance around and notice his cabin is completely bare of any sort of holiday spirit... typical bachelor stuff. "I don't suppose you have a tree we can decorate?" I ask hopefully. "I brought a small fake one, but it would be so much better if we had a real one. Is there any place around here to buy one? It would mean the world to Sarah."

"How about a fresh cut pine tree?" He rubs the back of his neck, looking out the window at the snow coming down harder than ever now. "I might be able to find one out back, but not until the storm dies down."

"So, what do you usually do for Christmas?" I ask. He must not own any decorations, or they'd be out by now. When he doesn't reply right away, I remind myself not everyone celebrates Christmas. "I'm sorry. Are you Jewish?"

He smiles slightly and shakes his head. "No. I usually go to my mom's. Her place is always decked out for Christmas," he answers. "I would take you there to stay, but she's booked months in advance, and she doesn't have any beds available."

I'm torn and don't know whether to be horrified that we are at Matt's mercy for so long or just grateful. Hesitantly, I ask, "So, will you be okay with us staying here with you until my car is ready?" I just want to confirm what he told me earlier.

"Looks like it. Unless I can find another place for you to stay. But I have serious doubts that I will. This is the busiest time of year here."

The reality of our situation hits me, and I find myself on the verge of tears. I cover my mouth with my hand and quickly turn to walk over to the boxes and bins of decorations near the door that I brought. I bend over and fumble with one of them, trying not to lose it in front of someone I don't know.

But Matt notices. When I glance back at him, his eyes are full of sympathy. I know it isn't his responsibility to provide us with our dream Christmas, but I planned this for so long, and I don't want to disappoint Sarah. I clear my throat and, in the absence of anything else to say, tell him, "Thanks for letting us stay."

He walks over, and at first, I think he's going to reach out for me. Take me in his arms and give me a comforting hug. Not from any creepy motivation, but because I probably look like I need a hug right now. Instead, he hesitates for a moment next to me and then continues on to the hearth. "I'll get the fire started," he says, crouching down next to the iron log rack and grabbing some wood and kindling to stack in the fireplace grate.

I have a gas fireplace at my house that I can turn on with a phone app. In fact, I can control just about everything from my phone—lights, heat, stove.

I watch as Matt kneels in front of the fireplace, carefully rearranging the logs. He lights a match, holding it close to the kindling, and it ignites within seconds. The fire grows, flames flickering and dancing, casting shadows on the walls and filling the room with the scent of burning wood.

Despite myself, I feel my worries lifting, and I begin to smile. It is just what I envisioned for our stay at the other cabin.

Matt stands up and brushes his hands off. "There we go," he says, gesturing toward the crackling fire that seems to have gained a foothold on the dry wood of the logs. "That should warm things up a bit."

Matt disappears down the hall to change out of his ski clothes, then returns wearing a blue shirt and a pair of faded blue jeans. His sleeves are rolled up, revealing a set of muscular forearms covered in light hair—and are those tattoos? I stand up from the boxes of decorations. I'm not going to do anything with them tonight, so I move slightly closer to him under the pretext of unpacking the boxes of food in the kitchen.

Before I can get a better look, Matt's phone rings. He hurries off to retrieve it from a table near the door. With one hand over his ear and the other cupping the phone next to his face, he turns toward the window, facing outside. I start to pull out what we brought—cereal, boxes of mac'n'cheese, two loaves of bread—but I make out bits and pieces of his conversation despite the low tone of his voice.

"Sorry, I need... cancel... another time... after snow lets up." He ends his call and joins me in the kitchen.

I feel even more awkward after overhearing some of Matt's side of the phone call. "Are we interrupting something?"

"No, don't worry about it." He smiles at me but changes the subject. "I put a stew in the Crock-Pot before I left to go skiing, so that will be dinner tonight. Can I get you anything to drink? I have some cider that I can heat up and add some brandy. Or red wine. A hot chocolate for the kiddo when she wakes up? You just name it."

"Thanks, spiked cider sounds perfect." I need a drink after everything that went on today.

Right on cue, I hear a sleepy, "Mommy?" from the living room. Sarah's little head pops over the top of the couch, yawning and rubbing her eyes.

I hurry over. She's pretty independent for a five-year-old and rarely gets upset when I'm around, but this has been an eventful day for both of us. She seldom naps anymore, and to fall asleep in a car and wake up in a strange house might be a bit of a surprise for anyone.

I sit down on the couch, and she snuggles sleepily against me for a moment and gives me the hug I needed. But before I know it, she's wiggled out of my arms and was exploring the living room like a curious cat. When she sees Matt getting mugs out in the kitchen, she tugs at my arm and whispers, "Mommy, can I have hot chocolate? With marshmallows? Pleeeeeease?"

I smiled down at her. "Of course, sweetie." I'm glad I brought marshmallows because I doubt Matt has any in his cupboard.

Matt calls out, "Sure thing, Sarah." He pulls milk from the fridge, and I head over to help him get our drinks ready and to put away the rest of our food supplies. The two of us work in companionable silence while Sarah putters around the living room, picking knickknacks up to look at—Matt has a collection of carved, wooden animal figurines scattered throughout the room—and putting them down again after petting them, just as if they were real animals.

Well, this is where we are going to spend the next two weeks unless we can find another place to stay. I hope Matt won't get too annoyed by our presence here.

Matt gets Sarah her hot chocolate, and then hands me a mug that has writing on it. I lean against the counter and take a sip before I read what the mug says and almost choke. I held it up to show him and raise my eyebrows. "Behind every great man... is a woman rolling her eyes?"

He starts laughing involuntarily, and I can't help but smile. With his eyes crinkling at the corner like that, he is kind of cute. "My sister gave that to me," he replies.

I nod and sip my cider as Matt gets out bowls and takes the lid off his slow cooker, releasing a cloud of steam and the delicious smell that has permeated the kitchen. He fills the bowls up and carries them, along with spoons, over to the table.

Drinking my cider and watching Matt, I wonder about him. I like the way his eyes sparkle, and his hair falls across his forehead, barely brushing his eyebrows. Now that we're inside and I have time to examine him, and I wonder how old he is— 30's maybe or older. His beard hides what is probably a nice looking face. Why is a man like him living alone here in this mountain town? Maybe he's divorced.

He motions for us to come to the table to enjoy the beef stew. We all sit down, and there's a bit of passing of bread and butter to enjoy with our meal.

"Do you live here full time?" I took a bite of the stew. The meat is tender, the potatoes soft and filled with flavor. "Mmm," I add appreciatively. Cute and can cook? He must be a unicorn.

Matt nods, his mouth full. He swallows and takes a sip from his mug. "Yes, I do. I run a construction company with my brother."

I raise an eyebrow, impressed. "Hard work. But it must be rewarding to see the results of your labor."

"It is," Matt agrees. As he speaks, my eyes drop to his large and capable hands, and I can't help but notice a few scars on their backs, a pale white against the parchment tone of his skin. "I enjoy doing something physical and working with my hands. It's satisfying to build something from scratch. However, these days, I spend a lot of time on the various sites supervising a crew."

I take another spoonful of stew and feel a little envious of him for being able to get outside every day. "I sit at a computer. Pretty boring."

Matt grins. "Always glued to your screens and gadgets instead of enjoying the great outdoors?" He shakes his head. "Definitely not for me."

"There is a lot you can do in the city," I point out. It's not until the words leave my mouth that I realize they sound defensive.

He must have heard it, too, because he cocks his head to the side and gives me a penetrating stare. "Don't you get tired of the city life? The noise, the pollution, the crowds? Not to mention all those strangers." He sips from his mug and then adds, "It's so impersonal. Do you even know your neighbors?"

I shrug. "Well, yeah."

When Sarah looks up at me—having shredded her slice of bread all over her bowl of stew and herself—and asks, "Who?"

I feel a bit silly. I amend my answer to, "Some of them." Then, at my daughter's continued stare, I say, "Maybe. But I love the convenience. Everything is right at my fingertips. Plus,

I get to try different restaurants and go to the park and the Saturday markets. I can walk or take an Uber or bus to most places. There is so much to do. Museums, art shows, the theater."

"I suppose that's true, if you like that sort of environment and that fast pace of life."

My turn for the interrogation. "Don't you get bored out here in the middle of nowhere?"

Matt leans back in his chair, crossing his arms over his chest. "Are you kidding me? There's always something to do or see."

"Like what?"

The smile on Matt's face widens. "Great hiking trails throughout these hills. Not to mention, it's ski and snowboard season now. In the summers, we take the boat out on the lake and do some fishing. Or if you're feeling adventurous, you can raft down the river or do some hunting in the fall." He nods his head at Sarah. "Great place for kids to grow up."

There is that. I look at my daughter, who is busy shoveling buttered bread in her mouth. Some stew made it in there, too. But she's not a fan of things that are too chewy, according to her, like slow-cooked meat.

I glance back at Matt and nod, but I can't get beyond the picture of spending just a week in the summer at a cozy cabin surrounded by nature. That would be ideal, a short vacation here. But I'm still not so sure about living in a place like this full time by myself.

"But what about the lack of convenience?" I ask. "How do you cope without department stores or Trader Joe's? Does Amazon even deliver here?"

Matt chuckles. "We aren't as backward as you may think. Yes, Amazon comes here. There are excellent restaurants in town and a lot of seasonal activities that bring people from all over the world."

I nod thoughtfully. "Okay. But you still have to drive everywhere."

Matt shrugs. "It's all about priorities. For me, the mountains are where I belong. I wouldn't trade it for anything."

Once we finish eating, since he doesn't own a dishwasher, I help Matt with the dishes. He washes, and I dry while Sarah colors in a book we brought along for the trip. Right when we finish, I yawn. I'm dead tired, and I expect that, despite the nap, Sarah will be as well.

Matt notices. "I'll show you to your room," he says as he pulls the plug on the soapy water in the sink to drain. He leads me the short distance down the hallway and gestures through the open door of the bedroom I had snuck a peek at before.

"I hope this will be okay for you and Sarah," he says, pushing the door open further. "It's not much, but it should be adequate for your time here. Don't want you to get too comfortable, or I'll have to kick you out." His eyes are doing that crinkling thing at the corners again as he smiles at me, and I feel a flutter in my stomach that I firmly ignore.

"It's perfect," I say, stepping inside. I notice a queen-sized bed with a handmade quilt across the top and a dresser against a wall. He flicks a switch on the wall, and a small lamp brightens the space, providing a soft, warm glow around the room to give it a cozy feel. "Thank you so much."

"I'll go put fresh towels in the bathroom for you and Sarah to use," he adds.

"Thanks." As he heads to the bathroom to get us our towels, I return to the front to grab our suitcase to bring back to our room.

When I hear Matt's footsteps retreating to the kitchen, I go to the bathroom and look around. There is a shower and a decent sized counter around the sink. There's not enough room for all my toiletries, though. *Not staying in a hotel*, I remind myself. With a touch of amusement, *We're really roughing it now.*

I get Sarah ready for bed and tuck her in with a kiss, turning off the light before going to brush my own teeth. As I emerge from the bathroom, I hear a noise behind me and turn to find Matt standing there. His blue eyes are making a slow journey of me from head to toe, and they widen just a little as they go.

Looking down, I suddenly feel self-conscious. I'm used to it just being Sarah and me. I forgot to pack a robe and am wearing my reindeer leggings and a cropped T-shirt that exposes my belly button and ends just below my chest.

He averts his gaze and clears his throat. "Sorry. I didn't— Uh, let me know if you need anything."

"I'm fine," I say, my voice unsteady. His gaze was almost as strong as a touch, and now I feel as unsteady as my voice. It has been years since I lived with a man, and I've forgotten just how intimate a thing it is to share a space. "Just getting ready for bed."

Matt nods, still avoiding eye contact, and backs away slowly. "Right. Well, I'll leave you to it then. Goodnight."

"Goodnight," I say while watching him disappear down the hallway back to the living room.

I feel a twinge of embarrassment. Even if only for a short time, I suppose I'll need to get used to living with a strange—a really attractive—mountain man.

Chapter Two

MATT

The light is soft and diffuse in the morning as I peer outside through the frosted windowpanes of my bedroom. Snow is piled high against the walls of the cabin. I make a mental note to myself: later, I'll need to clear a path to the trail out back for Paige and Sarah.

After I get dressed in a flannel shirt and jeans, I head down the hall to start a fire in the living room and put coffee on. I guess it's pancakes for three this morning.

Before I've even started mixing the ingredients I've piled up on the counter, Sarah wanders over and plops a stuffed bear on the table. She's wearing red pajamas covered in Elf on a Shelf characters posing in all sorts of funny ways. She glances up at me and says, "Hello."

I return her greeting, bemused. That's all the permission she needs to clamber off with her bear and begin an imaginary game with him that involves some of the wooden animals in the living room. Keeping half an eye on her—I'm not worried about her breaking anything, but some of the carved creatures are somewhat heavy and won't feel good dropped on a toe—I pull out mixing bowls and a wooden spoon and turn back to the counter.

That's when Paige appears with the knitted throw my mom gave me wrapped around her like a giant shawl. I can see her reindeer leggings sticking out the bottom, and fuzzy slippers covering her bare feet. Her shiny blonde hair is held back with a clip.

"Do you have an espresso machine?" she asks sleepily as I crack more eggs and begin to whip up some pancakes. Behind me, on the stove, the scrambled eggs start to sizzle in the frying pan.

My immediate reaction is to chuckle at the city girl. "Espresso? Sorry, all I've got is plain coffee. The nearest Starbucks is a good twenty miles away." I stir together flour and baking powder, then add the mix to the eggs and milk.

She frowns. "Please tell me you have coffee creamers? I hate black coffee."

I drop some circles of batter onto the hot grill before I open the fridge and pull out a carton of milk. "This should do the trick." Then I grab a packet of sugar from a bowl on the counter and hand it to her. At her disappointed expression, I remind her, "It's not fancy, but it's better than nothing."

"I guess this will do. Thanks." She ties a large knot in the throw to keep it from slipping off so she can use her hands.

I raise an eyebrow and cross my arms, leaning back against the counter. If she's expecting to be served, she will have another thing coming. "I'm no fancy chef either. I've got pancakes and eggs."

She raises her eyes from her coffee cup and gives me an apologetic smile. "I'm totally *not* a morning person. Rudeness is my middle name before I get caffeine into my system."

Paige pours the milk and adds the sugar to her mug, giving

it a brief stir with a spoon. She must have fixed her drink to her liking because she takes several large gulps, closing her eyes in ecstasy and sighing. After a moment spent gathering herself, she looks back at me again. "Okay, I'm only half zombie now. Tell you what, maybe I can whip up breakfast tomorrow. Do you like crepes?"

I accept her peace offering with a teasing smile. "Hmm. Well, I might keep you around after all. At least you can cook."

She rolls her eyes at me. "Of course, I can cook. I wasn't planning on ordering takeout every day while we're staying here in the mountains."

I'm amused at her notion of being able to order takeout up here, away from town. I don't know how she would've fared if she'd chosen a better place to rent. I suspect she'd be driving into Leavenworth after a day or two looking for something to do.

"I'm hungry," Sarah says, adjusting her stuffed bear on the couch next to her.

"What about the bear? Would he like anything?" I ask. I like kids. They're simple and straightforward and tell you exactly what's on their mind. Most adults aren't so cool.

She picks up her bear and brings him over to the kitchen. "This is Teddy, and he only likes apples."

I check on the food, giving the eggs a quick stir before shutting off the heat. "I'm fresh out of apples. Maybe I can get some later for Teddy, if that's okay?"

Sarah looks at her bear, then back at me. She nods her head. "He says that's okay." She places him on a chair at the table, then comes back.

I stab a pancake and scoop some eggs and sausage onto a plate for Sarah. "Here you go, little missy. Chow down."

I put the rest of the pancakes on the table for Paige.

Holding the cast iron pan in one hand, I put two spoonfuls of eggs onto her plate, then dished up the rest to mine.

"I'm expecting a generous tip for my service." I grin, trying to make light of the situation.

"Oh, I'm sorry. Would you like me to pay you for staying here?" Paige's eyebrows go up.

Embarrassed, I quickly reply, "No, I was just kidding around. You don't owe me anything." After a pause, trying to regain the mood, "Except maybe a smile to start my day."

"Are you sure?" She takes a bite of her eggs.

Man, if there was ever a misunderstanding—this is the difference between small towns and city folk. City folks think they can solve everything by buying it. "Yes," I reply shortly, hoping to close down the subject.

"Are we going to get a tree today?" Sarah asks, her eyes wide with excitement.

Saved by the bell. Although her question seems to be directed at her mom, I answered Paige. "A little later, if the weather permits."

Paige gives me a relieved smile. "Thank you."

I watched as Sarah digs into her pancakes, chattering about her favorite book that has a giant red dog in it. Her teddy bear has moved up from the chair and is now propped up against her plate. Paige sips her coffee, looking around the room with interest.

This is totally new to me, and I'm caught between the unreality of this domestic scene compared to how I usually begin my days. I've rarely have a female spend the night here, and I've never dated anyone with a kid. I always thought I would have a family with a house full of noisy children running around like the home I grew up in. But since the only woman I ever wanted to start a family with hated the idea, I've gotten used to believing that it might not be in the cards for me.

I steal glances at Paige as we eat, admiring the twin dimples that peek through when she laughs at something Sarah says. I try to focus on the conversation, but I keep wondering what it would be like to be with someone like her instead of the women I normally date. What kind of man appeals to her?

She probably goes for those rich guys that can take her out and drop a bundle on a fancy meal, I think in disgust. Exactly the opposite sort of lifestyle I'm interested in. Being the half owner of a booming construction business, I'm not exactly poor myself, but you wouldn't know by the house I live in. I keep a low profile and enjoy a simple life in my cabin. I'd always had plans to someday build a nice house for myself with a view, like my brother Grady and his gal Jess have. But that was when I thought I would have a family and a wife. A big place makes no sense for a bachelor. What would I do with all that space? I'd rattle around it like a pea in a pod.

Well, those are just ideas out there in the future. Unfortunately, they get further away as every year goes by. These days, I'm not into long-term relationships. Certainly not with any of the women I've met around here. Maybe I'm too picky or just never met the right woman, which is fine for now. I can't complain.

A pang of annoyance washes over me when Paige and Sarah walk into the kitchen an hour or so later, telling me they're ready to adventure out to get a tree. My eyes scan Paige's outfit, and I can't believe what I'm seeing. The short sweater she has on is a bright robin's egg blue, and it looks like it would be soft and warm to the touch. It has a rounded neckline that exposes her collarbones and hints at the form underneath. Her black leggings hug her curves but offer no insulation or waterproofing. She's wearing the same pair of bright yellow rubber boots from yesterday. The wool coat she brought with her may be stylish and hugs her admittedly very nice figure, but it is little more than a thin layer of fabric.

Their clothing is clearly not suitable for the harsh weather outside. "You've got to be kidding me." I blurted out. "You're not planning on wearing that into the snow, are you?" I gesture toward the window. "Those rubber boots are no protection from the cold. And that *coat*." I shake my head.

Paige looks down at her outfit, but her expression is challenging when she meets my eyes. "It's all we have. I didn't realize I needed to shop at REI before we came on this trip."

I let out a deep breath. I shouldn't be so hard on her. She's just a clueless girl from the big city and doesn't know any better. It irritates me she hasn't prepared better for the weather, especially since she has Sarah with her, but being out here must be outside her wheelhouse. Perhaps I could show her the basics, so she won't be caught unprepared next time she decides to venture out into the countryside. Of course, that's assuming she ever does so again.

I go to my closet and begin rummaging through my old winter clothes. Although she's half my size, I have a few extra jackets and a sweater. Perhaps they will work well enough. After a few minutes, I found a pair of insulated boots I know are much too big. But if she wears several pairs of heavy socks, maybe her feet won't swim in them. There's also an old coat she can wear over my wool sweater and a pair of wool-lined gloves. Luckily, I found a cap with earmuffs to keep her head from freezing.

"Here," I say, handing them over. "These should keep you warm."

Paige slips on the coat. She's swimming in it, but at least it's better than what she brought. As she glances down at herself, rolling up the too-long sleeves and pulling up the zipper, I think maybe there's hope for her yet.

Until she wrinkles her nose and takes it off. "No offense, but I wouldn't be caught dead wearing this." She hands it back to me.

I guess my first impression of "city girl" was the right one. I know there's a scowl on my face when I tell her, "If you don't wear these items outside, you *may* end up dead in what you've got on."

She rolls her eyes, and it makes me think of the mug my sister gave me as a joke. In this case, I am one hundred percent certain that this woman will drive me crazy for the short time she's here, not be my inspiration.

"You'll just have to put fashion aside today while we get a tree and be glad you don't freeze your butt off in the process."

Paige crosses her arms and glares at me. "What about Sarah? Are you going to wrap her up in a bearskin?"

I glance over at the kid, who is looking between her mom and me as we spar as if it's a tennis match. I don't have any kid's clothes in my closet, so I have no idea how I'm going to remedy her situation.

As if clothes will pop out of the air, I scratch my beard and look around my small cabin. Then it hits me. "I might be able to find something in the attic. Give me a minute."

I go into the hallway and reach for the trapdoor in the ceiling to pull down the ladder. It's a steep climb, but I've done it before carrying boxes, so it's not so bad with my hands free. I pull the string hanging in the middle of the ceiling, and the bare lightbulb flickers to life and provides enough illumination to see by.

The space isn't too full, but it's dusty and has a number of boxes shoved against the outside walls. I crouch down and rummage through the boxes, wishing for the first time that I'd marked them better, until I find some old clothes that belonged to my nephew, Bobby when he was about Sarah's age. At the very bottom are the winter clothes, and I discover two woolen hats, one pair of matching gloves, a pair of bright blue snow boots, along with a faded cream snowsuit.

I scoop up the items and bring them back downstairs. When she sees what I'm carrying, Sarah's face lights up. "Are those for *me*?" she asks shyly.

Glancing up at her mom, I nod. I'm sure Paige thinks these are disgusting, too, based on the expression on her face, but she also doesn't seem to want to disappoint her daughter by complaining.

Sarah tries on the boots and stomps around the wooden floor, giggling. "These are so squishy," she says of the padded boots.

"What do you say?" Paige reminds her gently.

"Thank you, Matt." She stomps over to me, and I'm taken aback when she wraps her arms around my leg and gives me a quick hug. Without knowing quite what to do, I awkwardly reach down to pat her on the head.

For the first time since seeing my winter gear, Paige smiles at me. The expression lights up her face, and her dimples peek out again. Man, I'm a sucker for dimples. "Thanks, Matt," she says softly.

I clear my throat. "You're welcome." Paige even put the borrowed coat back on while I was in the attic. Now, they're both adequately dressed for the snowy outdoors.

"Where are we going?" Sarah asks eagerly, jumping up and down. "Are we going to see Santa? Are we at the North Pole?"

I chuckle. "It might *seem* like the North Pole here with all this snow, but we're still just in Washington."

"What are we doing?" A sudden thought occurs to her, and she dances from foot to foot. "Are we going to cut down a Christmas tree? Can we? Pleeeeease?"

"Sure, honey," I reply, as if it's all her idea. "Great thinking. We're going into the woods behind the house to find the perfect one."

When I see Paige flashing those dimples again, my stomach drops, and I have to glance away for a moment. I don't mind being cordial, but this is feeling a bit too chummy for my own good. It's not a surprise that, physically, Paige makes me sit up and pay attention. She's sexy as hell, the more so because she doesn't even seem to know it. But I can't understand why I'm feeling drawn to the whole package—this wholesome family scene. I decided long ago that I wasn't interested in something like this anytime soon, so God only knows why I find myself gearing the two of them up for an outing and planning to redecorate my whole place to suit them for the holidays. When it comes to our backgrounds and interests, this woman is definitely not my type at all.

As Paige and Sarah follow me out the back door, the chilly air nips at my nose and cheeks. I turn around to see if they are adequately bundled up and nod my approval as I see them tugging down their hats and straightening their gloves to protect their extremities. The clothes I've lent them will do the job well enough to keep them warm.

For some reason, I'm determined to make cutting down a Christmas tree in the woods a memorable experience for them.

I gather the supplies we'll need—a bow saw, gloves, rope, along with my wooden sled.

As we set off into the woods, Sarah is a bundle of excitement, chattering about decorating an actual tree for Christmas instead of a fake one. It's a beautiful day, and only snowing lightly. Earlier, I stomped out a path with my snowshoes for them to walk in so the snow wouldn't swallow them up to their knees.

Paige and Sarah trudge through the snow behind the sled. Their breaths puff out in little clouds of steam as we go. I'm grateful that they've taken my advice and dressed warmly; the winter weather can be brutal, even for those accustomed to it.

As we stroll along in the snow, I suddenly stop and hold up my hand. Paige and Sarah ramble to a halt behind me, and I point forward.

An elk is up ahead, with its ears perked up, but its head lowered as it mouths at something under the snow. I can tell the animal is male by its large and majestic antlers. Easily six feet at the shoulder and probably weighing in at over eight hundred pounds.

Sarah's voice is a loud whisper. "Can I pet it?"

"No, we need to just be still and watch. We don't want to scare it," I reply.

As Paige cautiously takes out her phone to snap some pictures, the elk raises its head and looks at us. Slowly stepping away and then picking up speed, the elk begins to move through the snow across the terrain, its long legs carrying it with grace. A moment later, it disappears into the woods.

"Wow. That was so cool." Paige beams. "I am putting those on Instagram." She tucks her phone in the pocket of the coat and puts her gloves back on.

I roll my eyes at the idea that Paige feels the need to

document everything. However, I'm glad at the same time, she can share photos of the elk with her friends. Seeing one is rare.

As we resume walking, my eyes return to scanning the woods for the perfect candidate for our Christmas tree. I pause at every pine, looking for a tall, bushy tree with a straight trunk and full branches for hanging ornaments.

"Aha!" I point to a tree off to the side of the path. "That might be the one. What do you think?"

Paige walks over, Sarah struggling in her wake. The snow here is deeper, and there are some drifts that have gathered against the edges of the trees. She walks around it with her hands on her hips and examines it from all angles. When she turns to me, she's smiling. "It's perfect," she says.

"Perfect!" Sarah echoes. She holds out her hands. "Can I cut it down?"

I chuckle. My sisters sometimes think I'm dense, but even I know better than to hand over a saw to a five-year-old kid. "Oh, I was going to leave that task to your mother." I held out the bow saw to Paige.

The expression on her face is priceless. "What?" she gasps at me.

"Too much of a softy to do any hard work?" I tease.

Her lips firm into a thin line. I chuckle as Paige takes the saw from me with a determined expression. "No way. I can handle it," she replies grimly.

"Watch out, we've got a lumberjack over here," I joke. I put my hands on Sarah's shoulders and gently steered her a safe distance away to watch her mom.

Paige positions herself in front of the tree, crouching down to figure out where to begin. My lips tremble, trying to withhold a smile. She has no idea how to hold the saw and ends up banging it to the side of the base with a resounding thud. The tree shakes, and a few needles fall to the ground.

"You're supposed to cut it, not slap it down." I can hear the laughter in my own voice, although I'm unwittingly impressed that she at least gave it a try.

Paige frowns, then hands the saw back to me. "Okay, Mr. Expert. Let's see *you* have at it."

I make quick work of taking down the tree while Paige gets in my face several times to snap photos with her phone. Sarah enjoys shouting "Timber!" at the top of her lungs as the tree comes down, and I laugh at her enthusiasm. With a few steps, I place our prize on the sled and start to pull, my two guests leading the way back home.

Chapter Three

MATT

I've never seen such excitement in someone's eyes when looking at a string of lights. But Sarah is doing a cross between dancing and jumping up and down. I don't remember the last time I laughed so much.

Paige hands me a string of lights. As I wrap them around each branch carefully, I hear Sarah giggling with joy as she lays out ornaments on my wooden coffee table. Paige has had to remind Sarah three times already that the lights go first because as soon as she turns her back, Sarah's hanging ornaments all around the bottom of the tree.

After I make quick work of the lights, I go to see what Sarah has put aside to decorate the tree with. She's cradling something precious in both of her hands, and she offers it up to me as if handing me a solid gold bar. It's a long, green ornament with a smiley face. I hold it up and can't help but chuckle. "What is this, Sarah?" I look down at her and raise an eyebrow.

She grins up at me. "Isn't it funny? It's a pickle!"

"It's funny, alright." I inspect the green thing for a moment before carefully putting it in the upper branches of the tree.

There are a variety of odd ornaments Sarah holds up to show me. "This one is a unicorn with a Santa hat!" she exclaims, holding up a rainbow-maned creature. "And this one is pizza! Isn't it silly?"

I smile at her enthusiasm but can't help but feel a bit confused by some of their Christmas decorations. A pickle with a smiley face? A llama with a present on its back? They all look somewhat ridiculous to me.

But Sarah doesn't seem to notice my amusement.

"This was my daddy's." Sarah holds one out to me with the navy emblem on it, placing it on my outstretched palm. It's a simple design with a bald eagle holding an anchor and "USN" above its head. US Navy. "It's my favorite."

I glance over at Paige. I admit that I've been curious about Sarah's father and why he isn't around. I don't feel comfortable enough to ask, especially with Sarah saying "was" when talking about her father's ornament. "Was" can be a pretty heavy subject when it comes to near-strangers, and I don't think Paige and I are much beyond that stage yet.

But the subject doesn't come up—at least, not with Sarah around. Paige sets her phone to blare old Christmas tunes, and we all sing "Rudolf the Red Nose Reindeer" and "Jingle Bells" while we work. They both have sweet voices.

I hang the higher ornaments while Paige and Sarah hang the lower ones. As we work together, it takes me back to my childhood and the fun I had as a kid decorating the tree with my siblings. After I bought this place, I had no reason for a tree or any decorations since I lived here by myself. Who will be there to see them? And my mom always goes overboard with

Christmas and a party every year. I find that to be enough holiday spirit for me.

As we finish hanging the last ornament, we step back to admire our work. The tree looks stunning, decorated with the multitude of colors and shapes—from the silly ornaments to more traditional lights and bulbs. I go get my ladder, climbing up, and then proudly place the star on top of the tree. I grin down at Paige, who is kneeling down with her arms wrapped around Sarah from behind, smiling back up at me. For one quick moment, my heart thumps too quickly in my chest.

I climb down and put away the ladder before I turn off the overhead lights. The room is now illuminated by the soft glow of the tree, creating a magical ambiance in my otherwise dull living space. I feel like singing again like a little kid, but I bite my tongue against the impulse before I became as cheesy as a Hallmark movie.

After dinner, I head down the hallway to get to my shop when Sarah appears in front of me holding up a book with two hands like she's a crossing guard holding up a stop sign.

"Can you read me a story?"

"Wouldn't you like your mom to read it?"

Sarah grabs my hand and leads me back to the living room. "No, I want you to read it."

I sit down on the couch. Sarah plops down next to me.

Sarah opens the book and points to the page. "This is where Mommy left off."

I begin with a voice filled with intrigue, "And so Zondra, the brave little girl, ventured into the enchanted forest, determined to save the kingdom from the terrible dragon..."

"Is the dragon really big and scary?"

I smile. "Yes, Sarah, but Zondra is brave and smart. And sometimes, that can help you overcome the biggest challenges."

Sarah nods. "I wanna be brave and smart like her!"

"I bet you will be, kiddo."

I notice Paige tiptoeing into the room, phone in hand, ready to snap more photos. I ignore her and continue reading, "As Zondra walked deeper into the forest, she discovered a magical, talking tree that offered her advice on how to defeat the dragon."

Sarah crosses her arm with one hand raised up to her face and taps her lips with one finger in an oddly adult pose that looks funny on her. It's either natural, or she saw it on TV— I'm guessing TV. "Are there talking trees in your forest?" she asks.

I laugh. "Maybe. I've never met one, though."

I look up at the phone pointed in my direction. "I hope you don't mind that we started story time without you," I say, wondering when Paige is going to put her phone down.

Before Paige can answer, Sarah tugs on my sleeve. "What happens next, Matt? Does Zondra beat the dragon?"

"What do you think?"

"Of course, silly. She's the good guy."

"So, you know the ending?"

She shakes her head.

I set the book down. "Maybe we can read the rest later."

I think the little girl will protest, but instead, she scoots closer and cranes her neck to look up at me. "Why do you have all that hair on your face?"

"Oh, you mean this glorious masterpiece?" I stroke a hand down my mustache and around my mouth to my beard like an evil villain. "It's part of my rugged charm. Plus, it keeps my face warm during these cold months."

I hear a quiet chuckle behind me. "Rugged charm? Is that

what they're calling it these days? I was thinking more along the lines of 'lumberjack chic.'"

"Are you making fun of lumberjacks?" I turn around, resting one elbow on the back of the couch so I can look at her. Of course, as soon as I do, she snaps a picture, and I try not to flinch. I'm not camera shy by any stretch of the imagination, but I'm not a fan of always having a screen in my face. "They happen to be strong and muscular, so I'll take that as a compliment."

"Well, I suppose there are worse things than being compared to a lumberjack. At least you've got the flannel shirts to match." Finally, the phone goes away in the back pocket of her jeans, and she walks around the couch to settle on the chair on the other side of the coffee table. I look pointedly at the empty space between me and Sarah, but she just shrugs and doesn't get up to join us.

I rub my hand along my beard again and wiggle my eyebrows at her in an exaggerated leer. "A lot of ladies like beards. They think it makes a man look sexy."

"Really?" She snorts. "Well, *I've* never found them to be sexy. I'd never kiss a man with a beard. I'm afraid I'd get a road rash on my face if I did."

"It's very soft. Not rash-causing at all." I turn back to Sarah, who has been inching closer to me as I speak to her mom. She obviously has a mission in mind, and I give in pretty easily. "You want to feel it?" I offer.

She doesn't need to be asked twice. She reaches over, and her small hand pets my hair like she's trying to flatten it. "It feels like Susie's dog." She leans back again, mission accomplished.

Laughing, I turn to her mom and say, "You know, Paige,

since you're so curious about the beard-kissing experience, there's only one way to truly find out how it feels."

Paige raises an eyebrow. Her expression is a cross between the verge of laughter and a scowl. "What do you mean by that? Is that a dare?"

I grin. "Well, you could always give it a try. You know, for the sake of scientific inquiry."

"Kiss him, Mommy." Her daughter giggles.

"Sarah, you stinker. And you—you—" She obviously can't think of a word strong enough with her daughter there. "Matt. You must be pretty confident in your beard's ability."

I put my hands behind my head and lean back, enjoying the banter. "I'm just saying, if you're curious, you might want to try it out. Who knows, you might even enjoy it. Won't be able to get enough of it. And then I'd have to hide from you before you wore me out with your kisses." I try to keep my tone light, in keeping with the atmosphere, but it's hard to.

Well, until Paige bursts out laughing.

"I'll keep that in mind. But for now, I think I'll stick to the thrill of wondering." She smirks at me and then motions to Sarah. "Come on, it's your bedtime."

After all the tooth brushing and goodnights and hugs and glasses of water required to get Sarah tucked away into bed, I bring out a bottle of wine. Paige has moved to the couch, and I step in front of her. "Would you like a glass? It's from my brother's winery."

Paige nods her thanks, and I uncork the bottle. "You have a brother?"

"Three, actually, and two sisters." I pour her a glass and hand it to her before settling in next to her—but a safe distance away. I truly don't think there will be any more beard petting tonight, even if it's innocent.

She accepts it and takes a sip. "Do they all live around here?"

"Yep. So does my mom. Though my older brother tried to ship mom off to an old folks' home a while back."

Paige looks at me abruptly. "Is she okay?"

"Oh, yeah. She ended up turning our family home into a bed and breakfast." I take a sip of my wine. Without looking at her, I add, "I'm glad we finally get to spend some time together tonight, just the two of us."

I'm still looking away from her—nominally into the fire in the fireplace—but I know my words are loaded, especially when there's a moment of silence before Paige responds. "Yes, having a kid takes up a lot of time."

"So, tell me about your family. Do they live around here?" I sip my wine.

"Oh, no, my parents died years ago. I was an only child, so it's just me and Sarah."

I turn my head to look at her. "I know it's none of my business. But where's Sarah's father?"

Paige takes a deep breath before speaking. Her voice is soft. "He was killed in Afghanistan. He was a Navy SEAL," she says. This time, it's her gaze fixed on a distant point. "Skip and I were high school sweethearts, inseparable until graduation. But after that, we went our separate ways. I pursued my passion for computer science at college, and he joined the Navy."

Paige is quiet for a moment. "By some stroke of fate, we ran into each other years later and ended up getting married. I had no idea what it would be like to be married to someone in the military who was deployed for months at a time. I was lonely, but managed. After Sarah was born, it was especially difficult. He was gone all the time."

Paige's eyes glisten in the light of the fire, and she blinks rapidly for a moment and looks down at the glass she's holding in her lap. "I was devastated when I got the news that he wasn't coming back. It was like the world stopped turning. Sometimes, it feels like it all happened so long ago, but at other times, the pain is there, just as raw as ever. Sarah was just two years old. She barely remembers him. But I still try to keep his memory alive for her."

I notice our knees are touching, just on the edge. I can see the pain etched on Paige's face, and I regret bringing up the subject. This is much heavier than I meant it to be.

"So, have you dated anyone special since?" I ask, trying to keep my tone light.

Paige's expression changes at my question, and I feel a pang of guilt. I shouldn't be asking about her dating life. It's none of my business. But before I can apologize, she answers.

"No," she replies. Her voice is practically a whisper. "I'm not into... casual."

I nod, realizing how insensitive my question may have sounded. "I'm sorry. I didn't mean to pry."

Except I did. Even only knowing her for barely twenty-four hours, I can tell Paige is a strong, caring woman. While we speak, I can't help but keep stealing glances at her. Her every movement is graceful and effortless, and her presence in my house captivates me. I'm drawn to her in a way that has nothing to do with how beautiful and sexy she is. I've never experienced anything quite like this before. Listening to the story of her one true love makes me feel jealous and small for wishing she'd talk about me like that, and I've never felt that way about anyone.

I sigh, telling myself this is just a temporary attraction that will fade once Paige leaves. And she *is* going to leave—of that, I have no doubt. There's nothing to keep her here. She really doesn't belong in my small cabin near a tourist town. From the top of her highlighted hair to her designer jeans, she sticks out like a sore thumb to the locals.

When she begins speaking again after a long pause, I'd almost forgotten the unanswered on my mind. *Oh, right. Sex after being widowed.*

"Most men aren't excited about dating someone with a five-year-old daughter. And I need to be careful. I don't want Sarah to get attached to someone and then not have the relationship work out."

"I can see that would be a problem." I almost regret starting this conversation. I wanted to know her past, but there was nothing I could do to make her feel better. Although, at the same time, I want to offer her some comfort. "You're a great mother, Paige. I'm sure you'll find someone thrilled to be in your life and Sarah's."

Paige smiles again, but I can see the sadness lurking behind her eyes. "I hope so," she says softly. "But for now, Sarah is my priority. I just want to make sure she's happy and safe." After a pause, she looks over, her eyes curious. "What about you, Matt?" she lobs the question back at me. "Have you ever been married?"

I take a deep breath—and a big gulp of wine—before answering. "I was engaged once," I tell her. "But I called it off. I realized she wasn't the person I wanted to grow old with."

Paige nods sympathetically, and I continue, "My ex-fiancée and I had different ideas about our future. She didn't want a family, which surprised me. I always pictured myself as a father someday, and I was disappointed to find out she didn't want kids." I'm not about to reveal that when Laurie discovered she was pregnant with my child, she had an abortion. When she told me afterward, I was crushed that she never even discussed it with me.

"That must have been a shock."

I try to make light of it but, whenever I think about how our relationship fell apart, it hurts. "Yeah. We met in Seattle while I was at the University. After college, I had plans to work in my father's business, but she wanted me to stay in Seattle and work for a firm there. My family was here, and we're pretty close. I enjoy living in Leavenworth, and I wasn't ready to just give it all up to please her."

"It sounds like you made the right decision. You would've resented her if you got married and moved away. Sometimes, you have to prioritize your own happiness and well-being over pleasing others."

I nod. "Exactly. And now, I'm happy with where I am in my life. I have a great job, a supportive family, and good friends. I'm not in a rush to get into a committed relationship just for the sake of it."

I don't look over at her, but I think we've both gotten the message loud and clear. She doesn't want to do casual. And I won't jump into a doomed, long-distance relationship. Despite the zing I feel every time I look at her, whatever we have here is over before it even starts.

"I'm going to bake cookies," Paige announces. She carries her empty wineglass into the kitchen and puts it on the counter by the sink. Then she strolls over to the pantry and pulls out the bag of flour she brought with her and begins assembling ingredients.

My phone rings. When I see who it is, I'm hesitant to answer, but I finally accept the call.

"Hi." Les's cheerful voice booms in my ear. "You want to come over for drinks? We can watch the new superhero movie tonight."

I look over at Paige. Finally, I reply, "I don't know."

"Are you coming or not?"

"I, humm... don't think I can. I have some unexpected guests right now."

"I've got a present for you."

I drop my head and whisper, "I told you not to do that." We were only casually dating and not exclusive at all, so I didn't think I needed to get her anything.

As if I never said a word, her wistful voice replies, "I miss you. Do you miss me?"

My throat tightens, and I avoid answering. Despite everything I've said to her—and everything she agreed to when we first hooked up—she's still looking for more than I'm willing to give. Heck, we've only gone out a few months.

"This isn't a good time. I need to go." I end the call before she can say anything else.

Paige looks up from her mixing bowl and notices my distraction. "Everything okay?"

I nod and try to sound casual. "Yeah, just a call from a friend. Nothing important."

I pour myself another glass of wine as Paige rummages around the kitchen for a cookie sheet. She carefully drops blobs of dough in neat, even rows and then places the sheet in the oven. It's a simple scene, but there's something about it that draws me in. Soon, the house is filled with the sweet smell of sugar cookies rising from the heat.

After several batches are done and resting on wire racks to

cool, Paige settles on the chair facing the TV. "Do you mind if I...?" Paige holds up the remote.

Shaking my head, I say, "Be my guest."

She grins. "I *am* your guest," she replies. "Do you like Christmas movies? There are some on Hallmark I've been wanting to watch."

Christmas romance movies, with their cheesy plots, are something I detest with every fiber of my being. "Great," I mutter to myself. This is getting a little *too* warm and fuzzy around here.

Once the movie begins, my collar tightens, and I pull on it. I don't have the stomach to watch this fluff. Suddenly, I'm feeling very claustrophobic. I enjoy spending time with Paige and Sarah to a point. But I'm missing my freedom and space.

I get up from the couch. "I'm going to go visit a friend of mine for a while." I feel a little guilty for leaving, but it isn't like I need to always hang around Paige and Sarah.

"Sure, don't worry about me. I'll be fine." Paige smiles and turns back to her film.

I text Les that I'm coming over after all. "Don't wait up," I tell Paige. "I don't know when I'll be back." I grabbed my coat and hat.

"Have a nice time," Paige calls out after me.

At times like this, I have mixed emotions about them staying there. They're taking over my house and my life.

Chapter Four

PAIGE

I awake to a thumping sound. I pull back the curtain and look out the window to find Matt chopping wood. He has a heavy, navy sweater on and the knitted hat he was wearing when we first met. Little white puffs of air escape his lips as he swings the ax high in the air and slams it into the wood, splitting each log into two. Then he tosses the pieces into a pile and grabs another log. I notice a cleared area around the house. The man was busy this morning.

I go to the kitchen and find the coffee machine on and some pancakes in the oven, warming. Darn. It was my turn to make breakfast. I'd promised the man crepes.

Sara comes running out of our bedroom in bright pink pajamas. "Hi, Mommy."

"Hi, sweetie." I dish up some pancakes and put them on a plate for her, carrying it over to the table.

She plops down in the nearest chair and I place the plate in front of her. She picks up a pancake in her fingers, tears off a piece, and sticks it in her mouth.

I shake my head at her. "Come on, Sarah. Use your fork."

She rolls her eyes at me but picks up the desired utensil and stabs at the remaining pancake. Before I can say boo, she's shoved a piece too large into her face, puffing out her cheeks and making her look like a chipmunk. I cover my mouth so my smile of amusement doesn't encourage her, but I know it's a losing battle.

Matt walks in with an armful of wood, which he sets next to the fireplace. He toes off his boots and strips off his sweater at the door. He's wearing a red and black flannel shirt underneath, once again making him look like a lumberjack.

"That should about do it for a couple of days."

I take out my phone and snap a photo of him next to the fireplace, running his hand through his hair.

"Do you think your phone has enough memory for all these photos?"

"Oh, hush. I'm just trying to capture my holiday stay. Plus, I might find some great shots for Instagram."

"You must have taken a hundred since you got here."

"You can never have too many memories, Matt."

"What are you taking photos of me for?" he asks as I scroll through my pictures. After a pause, he asks me with a sly tone, "Are you looking at them before you go to sleep every night?"

I glance up, scowling and ready to deny it, but realize he's only joking when he poses like a WWF wrestler and growls. I can hear Sarah giggling next to me as Matt strikes several poses, each one more ridiculous than the one before. I capture them on my phone. Even goofing off, I must admit he's sexy as hell. "Those are *so* going on Instagram," I threaten, laughing helplessly.

"Oh, no you don't!" he yelps, reaching for my phone. I hold it over my head, pretending to keep it away from him, but it's a hopeless battle. Not only am I still sitting at the table, but he's a zillion feet taller than me. He grabs it easily out of my hand. "Okay, then," he says. "Let me take one of you."

Crossing my eyes and sticking out my tongue elicits a groan from him. "Come on," he coaxes. "Give me a sexy look to remember you by."

I strike my best alluring pose. I can only hold it for a heartbeat before I burst out laughing. Sarah is giggling behind me too.

Matt raises his eyebrows. "What's so funny?" he asks.

"Oh, nothing." Now he has something to remember our stay here. I turn away, but I can hear the snap-snap-snap as he circles my daughter and me like paparazzi, taking picture after picture.

Sarah finishes her breakfast, and I send her off to get dressed. "Will you be going to work now?" I ask as he hands me back my phone.

"You better send me those," he warns and gives me his number to input into my contacts. I do, feeling a bit naughty as I send him the pics of Sarah and me. "No," he finally answers my question, "we closed the office for the holidays."

"Two things," I say.

He leans against the kitchen counter, arms crossed, and raises his eyebrows at me.

"First, I'm wondering if there's any way I can check on the progress of my car?"

"Sure, I can drive you to Leavenworth and show you around. It's a cute town. I think you and Sarah will enjoy it."

"That sounds wonderful. Second, I need to go online and figure out how to get my money back for that... that..." Words fail me. I'm always conscious of my daughter being around, but it ever there was a time for swearing, I think this would be it. "Well, that terrible guy who rented me the cabin." I wave my phone in the air. "I could do it on my phone, but I might have to print some receipts out after I get my money back."

He shrugs. "Sure, no problem. I have a computer and printer in my bedroom you can use. It's on the desk, so help yourself."

"Great. Give me about thirty minutes to get dressed and do the computer stuff, and then we can get going."

His eyes run over my pajamas, and the slight heat in his lidded gaze makes my stomach jump. "You'll be able to buy some better winter clothes too. Maybe some that actually fit this time."

* * *

I can't believe it. Am I dreaming? My mouth must be hanging open as I crane my neck to take in all the details of this Bavarian town.

It's like driving into a movie set. The trees and gazebo are decorated with twinkling lights. Giggling kids are sledding down a small hill in the middle of town. The half-timbered shops along the main street are painted in bright colors and set off with decorations and bright lights.

I've never seen anything quite like it before. The town reminds me of a miniature German or Swiss village someone puts out every year for Christmas. The streets are white and sparkling from snow, and tourists are wandering about dressed in colorful winter hats and scarves.

"Welcome to downtown Leavenworth." Matt smiles as he smoothly pulls his SUV into an open parking space and shuts off the engine.

"You're kidding me. This is your downtown?" I whip out my phone as I exit the car and begin taking pictures.

"Yes. My sister owns the shop over there." He points to a boutique on the main street.

Opening the side door for Sarah, I glance over where he's indicating. "She does?" Then I unbuckle her so she can get out.

"Yeah. I'll introduce you. I'm sure she can help you find something to buy... whether you need it or not. But before you get too excited, I also want to point out some clothing stores. I don't want you to freeze your butts off every time you go outside."

"Lead the way." I take Sarah's hand.

His sister's shop is filled with a mixture of mountain décor and bright, colorful clothes. When we walk in, I notice a gal waving at Matt, then heading over in our direction.

"Well, who is this?" Her eyes go from Matt to me and Sarah like a ping pong match.

"Paige, I would like you to meet my youngest sister, Amber. She's the town's authority and busybody. So, I thought I would get it over with and introduce you before she started assuming things that aren't true."

I roll my eyes at the implication and stick out my hand. "Hello. Nice to meet you." Her handshake is firm as if she's used to being underestimated. I can respect that. After we shake hands, I place my palm on my daughter's head. "This is Sarah."

Amber bends over and solemnly shakes my little girl's hand, too. "Hello, Sarah," she says quite formally. It makes Sarah giggle, but she returns the handshake. Amber straightens up and turns to Matt. "These are the ones in need of a place to stay, I take it?"

He nods.

She turns back to me. "I wish I could help. Unfortunately, I don't have any room. But Matt will take good care of you.

Won't you?" Amber's face lights up in a huge grin as she talks to her brother. He scowls.

"Paige's car is being repaired. She and her daughter are just here for the holiday, then they're headed back to Seattle."

Amber shrugs. "Too bad you couldn't stay at Mom's. She really goes all out for Christmas. Maybe Matt could take you over there to see everything. I'm sure Sarah would love it."

"It's on the list," Matt mumbles.

"Well, I hope you enjoy your stay. Let me know if I can help you find anything in my shop."

Matt doesn't look like the type to hang around while we shop. I'm proven right when he says, "How about it if I meet you at the pastry shop over there in about an hour and a half?" He points down the street.

"Great."

The bell dings as the door closes behind him. Sarah becomes enraptured by some toys in the corner, and I sort through some of the handmade clothes calling my name. There are some I can wear back in Seattle, which is a bonus.

As I browse, Amber leans against the counter and watches me in a friendly way. "So, what do you think of my brother?" she asks, her tone a bit smug.

I smile, aiming for neutral. "He's been very nice to us. Though I hate imposing on him."

"Matt's a good guy. You're lucky he's letting you stay with him."

"Oh?"

"It's not like him to have overnight guests. He normally likes his space."

Hearing this makes me curious as to why he's so generous to us. While we've done a tiny bit of flirting, it's not been anything serious. I'm just visiting, and Matt made it pretty clear he has not interest in relationships... or big towns like Seattle. The flirting is just that... harmless and meaningless.

"He's been the perfect host so far," I reply noncommittally.

She grins. "Maybe he likes you."

I don't know how to respond to that except with the truth. "We're just here until Christmas, then he can go back to his routine again."

"Yes, he probably will." She sighs and straightens up. "Would you like me to ring those items up for you?"

Next, I pop into a boutique that sells children's items. Sarah picks out an adorable pink snowsuit and a hat to match that has two pompoms on top that look like ears. Pink mittens and insulated boots finish off her look. After making sure they fit, I let her wear them rather than the lightweight clothes she came into the store with. I don't know if she'll ever wear these again since we are only here for Christmas, and she's still growing, but I bite the bullet and buy them anyway. Although it's not urgent or necessary, I just have to get her two long-sleeved sweatshirts too. One with a moose on the front and another with a unicorn. To finish it off, I buy a pair of black sweatpants to wear inside Matt's house.

I'm feeling like I might have done okay and finished in plenty of time until I remembered I need snow clothes, too. It's not hard to find something in my size that's a cross between cute and functional, and I pick up a red ski parka, black ski pants, boots, gloves, and a hat that looks like a Tibetan mountain climber would wear. I change into these to surprise Matt when we meet him for hot cocoa.

We're headed in that direction when Sarah tugs on my sleeve and points. "I want to go in there." She pulls me inside a store filled with wooden nutcrackers of every figure and style, from the classic bearded red soldiers to a Santa Claus dressed in beach gear and with a pink flamingo perched on his stand. I ended up buying a classic nutcracker to take home as a souvenir.

I'm carrying so many bags that it feels like the circulation has been cut off in my hands, and I'm ready to sit down and enjoy something warm. The coffee shop is only half a block away, thank goodness, and Sarah is skipping with excitement over her cute new clothes.

A bell dings as we enter the coffee shop, and I wonder, half-seriously, if the bell over the door is standard issue from the mayor in this town when you open a store. It takes me a second to spot Matt, as he's not alone. There's a woman sitting with him who's quite attractive, with long, dark hair. She's just getting up as we enter the shop, and I wonder if this is another one of his sisters. They don't look alike, but you never know.

I get in line at the front counter to give Matt a moment, since it seems the woman is saying something to him. He stands up and helps her get her coat on. She picks up an open box and tissue from the table and stuffs it into her purse. He kisses her cheek, and she heads out the door without looking at any of the other people in the store.

Huh. Weird.

When we get to the front of the line, I order our drinks and some pastries, then we go to join Matt.

"Wow. Look at you two." He eyes Sarah up and down in her all-pink outfit. "Are you wearing cotton candy?" he teases her. She giggles. He glances up at me. "Seriously, that's a big improvement."

I set the shopping bags down and slide across from him. Sarah sits next to me.

"I thought since it's only a light snow and you looked

dressed for it, that we do a couple of things before heading back." Matt's attention is focused on Sarah.

"What are we doing?" Sarah's eyes widen with anticipation.

"First, we go to the reindeer farm so Sarah can see the deer, and then head over for a horse-drawn sleigh ride. What do you think?"

I think Sarah's going to burst with excitement. As for me, "Sounds terrific. I bet I can get some great photos to post on social media."

Matt doesn't bother to answer. "I checked on your car, and it looks like it won't be ready until Christmas Eve."

I give him a tight smile. "I hope you can put up with us until then."

"If not, I have a friend I can stay with."

Friend, hunh? I wonder if it was the woman he'd been talking to. "Sure, that sounds fine."

After warming up with our hot drinks and snacks, we drive a short distance to the farm.

Sarah is intrigued by the idea of the reindeer. "They kind of look like the elk we saw."

"They're relatives," he tells her.

"Do they fly too?"

Matt and I both laugh, and Sarah joins in, even though she doesn't get the joke. "I can't answer that," Matt finally replies when he catches his breath.

The sleigh ride is magical. The three of us huddle together under a blanket as the horses trot along a snow-covered trail. The experience feels right out of a fairytale, except with the reality of a cold and drippy nose, wind-slapped cheeks that are colder than cold, and numb toes. However, I know this is a memory that Sarah will never forget.

I shiver as the wind bites through me, even with my snow

clothes. Without putting it into words, Matt notices and puts his arm around me, pulling me closer to the heat of his body.

My stomach flutters at the feeling of his warm and comforting arm wrapped around me. I look over at him, and his eyes twinkle down at me, his smile almost too wide. He's obviously enjoying this as much as we are.

On the way back from the sleigh ride, Matt takes a detour back to town. So we don't have to cook tonight, he picks up a couple of to-go pasta dishes he ordered ahead from an Italian restaurant. Then, it's back into the warm car and the drive back to the cabin. Sarah falls asleep in the back.

I break the silence. "It was really nice of you to take us to see all these fun things today. I even have photographic evidence," I tease. "This is turning out to be a better time than I expected."

He smiles over at me. "I couldn't have you leave with a bad impression of Leavenworth."

"Thank you." I don't believe in knights in shining armor, but Matt is coming awfully close.

Chapter Five

PAIGE

"What are you doing?" I dash after Sarah, watching her disappear inside the room down the hall. "The door was shut, sweetie! What do I say about closed doors?"

Following her inside, it surprises me to see a large workbench loaded with all kinds of tools: knives, chisels, sandpaper, plus gloves, and a pair of goggles. There are bits of wood shavings and sawdust scattered over the table's surface, surrounding a roughly carved bird.

My mouth drops open at the sight. It's a workroom. I didn't know that Matt's a wood carver.

On one wall, hanging from hooks, are a variety of walking sticks in all shapes and sizes. A basket containing branches sits on the floor nearby. On another wall are carved ducks with cool designs and patterns lining the shelves. Some look very lifelike, while others have zigzag patterns or polka dots.

When I approach the workbench, I see a small notepad lying open next to the half-finished wooden carving. Flipping through the pages, I notice it's filled with sketches detailing different birds.

Sarah lets out a gasp, and my heart freezes as I quickly turn in her direction, afraid that she's hurt herself with one of these dangerous tools. But it's because she picked up one of the carved ducks and is inspecting it. I rush over to her and gently take the duck from her hands.

"These aren't toys," I warn Sarah.

She stares at me with a confused look, then sets the bird down. "But it's a duck."

"Matt made these for grownups."

She pouts, but I can tell she understands.

I hold her hand just to make sure not to get a scare like that again, and look closer at the walking sticks. I notice each one has a small carving of a bird or animal hidden in the handle.

"I didn't know Matt was so talented," I whisper to myself, but Sarah is the one who answers.

"He can make *anything*," she replies, her eyes bright with wonder.

Just then, the door is pushed farther open, and in walks Matt, looking surprised to see us in his workshop.

"What—what are you doing here?" he asks. He moved his gaze around his workbench, and I know he must be looking around to make sure nothing's been damaged.

"I'm sorry, Matt," I say. "Sarah wanted to explore, and I followed her in."

Matt's expression softens. "It's okay. Just—there are a lot of sharp tools here. Probably not the best place for a kid."

Sarah looks up at him. "I only touched the duck," she tells him. Then, when he gives a pointed look at the goggles still in her hand, she giggles and puts the hand behind her back.

"He's right, sweetie," I tell her, bending over her. I take the goggles from her and place them back on the workbench. "This really isn't for kids. Understand?"

She nods.

Behind us, Matt walks over to the table and runs a finger down the edge of his half-carved duck, examining it with a critical eye. "I've been working on this one for weeks," he says, his voice half-shy and half-filled with pride.

"It's beautiful," I say, meaning it.

Sarah has her arms crossed and her finger tapping her lips again. I know exactly what that means before she even asks. "Can you make me something?"

"Sarah!" I say. That one—give her an inch and she'll take a mile. She always manages to wheedle gifts out of strangers. I've had to have the "Don't take candy from strangers" talk with her more than once. "Matt's already been nice enough to let us stay here."

Matt bends down so he's face-to-face with Sarah. "What would you like?"

"A deer. Can you make me a deer?"

"I'm sure Matt is busy finishing up things he's making for other people right now." I don't want Matt to feel pressured. "You don't have to make her anything. I know you may not have the time."

"I do have one or two things to finish before Christmas."

I take Sarah's hand again. "We better go before my daughter steals one of your carvings."

"You wouldn't do that, would you?" he teases Sarah.

"Well..." She giggles and bobs her head up and down to say "yes."

"You will be in *so much* trouble if you do," I warn her. I turn to Matt. "I know this is your house, but maybe while we're staying here you could put a lock on the door high enough that Sarah can't reach it? I'm less worried about her taking a duck than an accident with the tools in here if she decides to sneak in again."

He nods. "You're right. I can do that."

I turn Sarah around by the shoulders and march her out the door.

As we return to the living room, I can't help but feel a sense of gratitude toward Matt. Not only has he taken us in, but he's also showing Sarah a lot of kindness.

"He makes cool stuff," Sarah says while twirling a lock of hair around her finger.

"Yes, he does." I still can't get over Matt making all those beautiful items. He has large, capable hands, but he never struck me as the creative type.

"I like Matt," Sarah announces as we sit down on the couch.

"He's a nice man."

"Mommy." Sarah tugs on my sleeve. "Do you think we could come back here next year?"

I smile down at her and give her a one-armed hug. "I think that would be lovely, sweetie."

Once I have Sarah settled in bed for the night, I take a book and return to the living room to read. I'm surprised to find Matt slipping on his coat.

"I'm going out."

Unlike most times we've spoken, his tone is short and brusque. It takes me aback for a second before I can respond, and I try to be as noncommittal as possible. "Good for you. You've been a terrific host, but I don't want you to feel like you need to entertain us all the time."

He nods. "I don't know what time I'll be back."

"Hey, I'm not your mother," I say flippantly, settling down

on the couch and opening my book with great and casual deliberation. "Stay out all night if you like."

Chapter Six

MATT

As I walk toward Les's place, the air is crisp and cold, and the sky clear. The smell of burning wood fills the air. The scent of pinecones and logs burning in the fireplace is inviting and familiar.

Les answers the door in a sexy getup that leaves little to the imagination—low-cut silk camisole with a lacy bra peeking over the edge, and tiny, silky shorts that reveal more than they cover.

"Damn, Les, you sure you want to be dressed like that on a cold snowy night?" I grin.

"Get in here," she says, yanking me in and closing the door.

I hang up my coat and pull off my boots before Les pushes me toward the couch. "I'm so glad you came over," she says. "Would you like some wine or beer?

"Beer, thanks."

Les leaves to fetch my drink. The room is dolled up in fancy Christmas decorations. In the background, I can hear the faint sound of holiday music.

It's nice to get out of the house. I was constantly playing

the role of a surrogate dad to Sarah, and boy, is she full of energy. I guess that's what I get for being a good guy.

For quite a while, I resisted dating Les. She'd been stalking me, hanging out at my sister's performances at different venues around town, waiting for me to show up. Kim knew Les had eyes for me and gave me a heads up. I finally gave in, knowing this would be only temporary. I'm not one for long-term relationships, and Les knows that. Or she ought to. It was one of the first things we both agreed on.

Les sashays back into the room and hands me a cold beer. I take a few long, cold swallows.

When Les settles down next to me, I put my beer on the side table and pull her close until she's in my arms. The smell of her perfume is alluring, and I nuzzle her neck. The feel of her hair against my cheek is a big turn-on. I press my lips to hers as my hands explore her curves.

I've been looking forward to tonight for a while. But the more I kiss her, the more I'm growing increasingly uncomfortable—and not in the usual good way.

So, I throw myself even more into it and push down that nagging feeling at the back of my head. Our kissing begins to grow more passionate, and I'm just about to suggest we take a trip upstairs when a full image of Paige's smiling face flashes into my mind.

My reaction is instantaneous; I pull back. Les tries to follow me and continue the kiss, but I place my hands on her shoulders to hold her in place. That tiny doubt that was worming around in my head turns into full-blown guilt. As much as I want to have something casual and fun tonight, I can't shake off the feeling of wrongness lingering in the back of my head. Les's eyes are filled with hunger, and her body's certainly ready and willing, but I can't go on.

"Matt?" she whispers.

I unwrap my arms from her and get up. I run my hands through my hair, but I can't tell her anything. Especially when I don't exactly know it myself.

"Are you not going to stay the night?"

I look over at Les. She's beautiful and alluring and wants me. But, somehow, it's not enough for tonight. Perhaps not for the future, either. My constant thoughts of Paige are making it impossible to focus on the woman who is right in front of me. "No, I'm sorry. Maybe another time."

Hastily, I put on my coat and head out the door, feeling a mix of regret and relief.

* * *

I flip on the light, and I see Paige still sitting on the couch, book trailing from her hand, with Sarah slumped in her lap, fast asleep.

Smiling, I hang up my coat. When I'd left, Sarah had already gone to bed. Obviously, something occurred while I'd been gone. "What happened?"

Paige looks like she's miles away in a place filled with peace and contentment. Sarah is curled up into a ball, with her small hands resting on Paige's chest. "Nightmare," she says. "She just fell back asleep, and I was thinking of carrying her back to bed before I dozed off myself."

I walk over and offer, "Why don't I take her? I can put her back to bed."

After a brief hesitation, Paige nods. I gently hoist the little girl into my arms and, without thinking, I place a kiss on Sarah's forehead as I'm walking her down the hall. A small smile forms on her lips as she begins to wake up.

She blinks up at me. "Hey," she says softly.

"Sorry to wake you."

"It's okay." She rubs her eyes. "What's going on?"

"I'm putting you to bed."

Sarah yawns and lets me tuck her into the guest bed. "G'night, Matt," she says before snuggling down.

I return to the kitchen to get something to drink; the door to the bathroom is closed, and I can hear water running inside. Then I head to my room.

I lie back on my bed with my arms behind my head, trying to think. The vision of Paige and Sarah on the couch plays in a loop in my mind.

I've never witnessed such a comforting vision before, and I'm reluctant to spell out why it was a relief to walk through the door and see the two of them there. Almost as if they were waiting for me.

Why, out of everything I've seen and done in my life, was that such a beautiful sight?

* * *

For once, Paige beats me to the punch, and I find some delicious crepes waiting for me the next morning. The meal is a little light for me, but I appreciate the effort she goes through to make breakfast.

I shake my head at the matching red Christmas sweaters both Paige and Sarah are wearing, covered in reindeers and green Christmas trees.

"Did you buy those in town?"

She grins at my expression. "Yes."

Smiling despite myself, I say, "I suggest you stay inside. I've got a few places to plow this morning, so I'll be gone most of the day. I don't want either of you to get lost in the snow while I'm gone."

Paige shrugs. "Don't worry—we'll be fine. See you later."

* * *

After dinner and cleaning the dishes that night, I announce, "I'm going to my shop to finish up some Christmas gifts. Hope you don't mind." I gesture at the living room. "Feel free to stream something if you're bored."

Paige barely looks up from her novel. "Sure, thanks."

I settle in at my table and begin sanding the duck I've been working on. What I love best about the craft is the feeling of the wood in my hands slowly turning from an inanimate block to a creation that almost feels alive to me. It's magical, and each creature comes from that starting point.

When I'm done sanding, I pick up a smaller piece of wood and begin whittling it into the shape. A couple of hours later, I realize I've been going for a while now and put my tools down, stretching the kink out of my back. Last night, I installed a slide lock on the outside of the door, and I make sure that it's latched before I head to the kitchen.

Yesterday, Paige and Sarah decorated the cookies she'd baked. I take a cookie from the plate and turn toward the living room. Paige is standing in front of me in her leggings and crop top.

"Sleeping with Sarah is a challenge. She hogs the bed at night." Paige yawns and stretches, reaching to the ceiling and exposing the smooth expanse of skin below her short T-shirt.

An unexpected rush shoots through me, and I try to push the feeling aside and focus on the cookie. But when she wanders past me, I catch a whiff of her scent—a combination of vanilla and spice. It's certainly more mouth-watering than the cookie I'm trying to eat.

Paige reaches around me to open the cupboard and take out a glass. She runs water into the glass, and I watch her drink, feeling thirsty myself. I look away, trying to calm the sudden rush of desire, until I feel Paige's hand rubbing an affectionate circle on my back.

"Thanks, Matt, for everything."

Our eyes meet. I give up and put down the cookie. "Paige, I'm sorry, but if you don't leave this room right now, I'm going to do something stupid."

"What?" Her brow furrows, but she doesn't remove her hand from my back.

Without answering, I bring my arms around her. The feel of her bare waist against my palms sends warmth running up from my fingertips and down to... other places. I lean over her, about to finally figure out what her lips taste like and release all the pent-up desire inside me. But before our mouths touch, I hear something that acts like a bucket of water on my libido.

"Mommy?" Sarah is standing there, looking up at us.

I immediately turn my head and drop my arms from Paige's waist.

"Yes, sweetie." Paige's face is bright pink. There's a slight smile on her face, but I can tell it's fueled by embarrassment.

Sarah pouts. "I woke up, and you were gone."

"I'm coming back to bed now. Why don't you go crawl under the covers, and I'll be right there?"

Sarah shuffles back down the hall with her stuffed bear dangling from her hand. I turn my attention to Paige and suddenly feel awkward. "I'm sorry. I don't know what I was thinking. I shouldn't have done that."

"Apology accepted." Paige turns and sets the water glass in the sink.

She has a slight smile on her lips as she walks down the hallway. "Goodnight, Matt," she says as she disappears into her bedroom.

I found Paige attractive since I first laid eyes on her, but tonight something shifted inside me. Maybe it's the way she speaks to her daughter with such love and tenderness, and it's hard not to want some of that. Or perhaps it's the way she looked at me tonight, her eyes filled with a mix of confusion and desire, as if she's feeling the same way I am.

Thoughts of Sarah creep in, and I realize I can't ruin everything for Paige and her daughter. I don't want to risk hurting either of them by my selfish behavior. I promise myself that I won't take this any further.

While I'm not heartless, my love 'em and leave 'em philosophy has never bothered me before. But, this time, there's more at stake. They're leaving soon, so while I would have welcomed something casual if she'd been open to it, there's no point in starting something that won't go anywhere.

I can't make her any promises, and she's not interested in anything less. And I know, having taken a good, long, hard look in the mirror—I'm definitely not the right man for her to pin her hopes on.

Chapter Seven

MATT

I'm in my shop working on the duck again. It's for my sister Amber for Christmas. It's wearing a hat and has a scarf around its neck. Amber likes odd things, so I know she'll appreciate this gift.

There's a knock on the door. Paige sticks her head in. "Is Sarah in here with you?"

"No, why?"

"It's probably nothing, but I like to keep tabs on her. I was busy doing the laundry, and I thought she was in the living room coloring, but she's not there."

"You sure?"

"Yes, I don't know where she could be hiding."

I set down the duck and leave the room to help search the cabin.

We both stand in the hall. I try to think of some places a kid could hide.

"Sarah," I call loudly, peeking in the hall closet.

After searching every room and not finding her, I begin

worrying. "You don't think she went outside by herself, do you?"

Paige's face contorts in panic. "She was asking about talking trees from the story the other night. She could've gone looking for one."

We dash to the hooks by the front door and notice Sarah's coat and boots are missing. I don't want to upset Paige, but if Sarah is out in the snow by herself, this could become pretty bad.

I grab my coat. "I'll go look for her."

"I'm coming with you."

"I don't want to have to worry about you out there too."

"I've got the right clothes now. And even if I didn't, you can't stop me. I'm her mom and I'm going out there."

I don't want to waste any more time arguing. "Okay, but stay close to me." I open the door and am immediately hit with the push of icy wind and snow. My adrenaline kicks in and my senses go on high alert.

"Sarah," Paige yells out behind me.

The snow is swirling in waves, and I know if Sarah is out there, she's probably cold and scared. "Stay here. I'll find her and bring her back." I slip on a pair of snowshoes.

"Matt?" I can see the fear in Paige's eyes.

"Just stay on the porch and call her name, so if she hears you, she'll know which direction to go in."

I step into the blast of swirling snow. My mind is racing with fear and worry. I need to find Sarah before hypothermia kicks in. Small bodies can get really cold, really fast.

Bending down, I search the snow for signs of footprints. This is my property and I know it well, but Sarah doesn't, and she's probably disoriented out here. It's too bad my dog Brewster passed last year. I miss the mutt. The guy reached the ripe old age of sixteen and had a good life. But without him, I'm searching blindly.

"Sarah," I yell again, then stop to listen.

The snow eats every sound. I try to think which direction she would have gone in, when I remember the path we followed to get the Christmas tree. It's a long shot, but it's all I have.

I haven't gone far when I find a soggy teddy in the snow, so I know I must be headed in the right direction. I shove it in my pocket and pick up my pace.

Finally, I hear what sounds like a high-pitched voice. As I break into an awkward run toward the sound, I recognize Sarah's voice yelling, "Mommy!"

I quicken my pace in the direction it's coming from. My heart is pounding in my chest. There are no lakes or ponds around here, no streams that wouldn't be frozen over. So, that's one less thing to worry about. But there's still a lot that can happen to a little girl in the middle of the woods. "Sarah, I'm coming!" I call out to reassure her.

Moments later, I find her sitting in the snow, wide-eyed and shivering, even with her jacket on. I scoop her up in my arms and hug her, probably too tightly. But I've never experienced such fear in my life before I heard her calling for help.

Knowing it might freak her out more, I try to keep the intense emotions I'm feeling from my voice. I unzip my jacket and pull her cold form against my body heat, holding the jacket closed around her as best as I can. Turning back to the cabin, I tell her, "We were worried about you."

"I got lost. The snow wouldn't let me see."

Knowing how differently this story could have ended, I held her tightly. "You're safe now. I'm taking you back home."

"What about Teddy?" She clings to me, and I can tell by

her shivering how cold she is. If we hadn't noticed she was missing when we did—Oh God, I don't want to think about it.

"He's in my pocket."

I deposit Sarah in Paige's arms when I reached the front door. They hug, and I can tell that Paige has been crying.

"Let's get inside so we can warm up."

Paige slips off Sarah's coat and boots while I kneel down and start a fire. I've never been so scared in my life. My heart is still pounding in my chest. The thought of finding Sarah frozen in the snow is unbearable.

Paige brings her daughter over to warm up by the fire, and she kneels next to me and rubs Sarah's hands. With a nod from Paige, I take over the task and gently examine her small fingers for frostbite. They appear cold but not damaged in any way.

Sarah suddenly lunges for my neck and gives me a tight hug. Tears well up in my eyes as I wrap my arms around her and hold tight. Over her small shoulder, my eyes meet the melting emotion in Paige's gaze, and it's all I can do not to say something I will probably regret. Something significant that I won't be able to take back.

I don't know when it happened, but this little girl means so much to me. I would have never forgiven myself if something happened to her.

Chapter Eight

PAIGE

Matt fixes us chicken soup and popovers for dinner, and we eat and eat and eat until I think our stomachs are going to burst. It's a relief to share such a normal activity together after the events of today. I feel wrung out like a washcloth.

A little while later, I tuck an exhausted Sarah into bed. She yawns, and then tells me, "Mommy, I left Teddy in the bathroom."

"You stay here. I'll go get him for you."

I shut the bedroom door and head across the hall. The door is closed, so I knock, but there's no answer. Sarah must have shut the door behind her—she sometimes does that at home. I can hear water running—she must have left the tap on, too. I better turn it off before Matt realizes we've emptied his water tank.

"Hey, Matt, are you in there?" I call through the door just in case I'm mistaken, but there's still no response. I glance over and see his bedroom door is closed, although he normally leaves it open—he must have retreated there after dinner.

Convinced with this final clue, I open the bathroom door

and walk inside. It takes exactly one and a half footsteps before my eyes catch up with my stride. As soon as they do, my heart skips a beat.

The room is warm and moist. Matt is standing in the shower with the water running down his chiseled chest and toned abs, steam billowing around him. His back is to me, and his muscles ripple in a *lot* of places as he reaches for the shampoo. I feel my cheeks flush as my eyes involuntarily travel over his body, and I bite my lip to stop myself from making a totally inappropriate sound in response to what I see.

But I'm frozen in place, and I can't seem to move my feet as my eyes follow his every movement like a thirsty woman in a desert. He squirts shampoo into his palm and lathers up his hair, each motion slow and sensuous. After he rinses off, he starts to turn around, perhaps sensing the open door. I quickly avert my gaze, completely embarrassed for intruding on his privacy.

"I'm so sorry," I stutter, backing up a step. "I didn't know you were in here."

"It's okay," he replies, seemingly unfazed by the situation. "I should have locked the door." Matt turns off the water and steps out of the shower, grabbing a towel. "Is everything okay?" His tone isn't smug, but I can tell he's not indifferent to my bright red cheeks.

Once the towel is safely around his body, I try to compose myself after I look up, but wow. Water drips down the sculpted muscles of his chest, and I'm starting to wonder things that I have no business wondering about. "Uh, yeah, I was just checking to see if Sarah left Teddy in here," I say quickly.

A smirk is developing at the corners of his lips and he takes one slow step toward me. There is a heat in his gaze that hadn't been there a moment before. "Enjoying the view?" he says, half-teasingly.

I stammer, my mind racing for a witty comeback, but I can't think of anything clever to say. Instead, I blush even more before my eyes drop down. I spy the bear on the floor and reach down to grab it as quickly as I can. Without saying another word, I flee the bathroom, racing back to the guest bedroom with Teddy in my hand.

His image is burned into my mind, and I can't stop thinking about him for the rest of the night. Seeing Matt in the shower is something I won't be able to forget anytime soon.

In the morning, Sarah is still asleep when I get up, probably still exhausted from her ordeal outside yesterday. I try not to wake her while I get dressed. When I walk into the kitchen, Matt is already there, looking a bit sheepish with a cup of coffee in his hand. I'm a little bit nervous about what to say. After all, I'd walked in on him in the shower last night. Even worse, when I realized he was in there, I hadn't been able to leave. I'd been frozen to the spot, unable to take my eyes off of him.

"I should have locked the door."

Before Matt can go on, I interrupt him, trying to make light of it. "Oh, don't worry about it. It's not like I haven't seen a naked man before."

When he realizes I'm not going to apologize—or run away in fear—a mischievous grin spreads across his face. "You could have fooled me. Your eyes were as big as dinner plates."

I'm sure my face is now beet red from his comment. "Okay, maybe I was surprised," I admit. But, even with the embarrassment, I can't keep a straight face.

After a moment of shared laughter, though, the mood turns somber. I can't help but notice how Matt is looking at me. It's as if he's seeing me in a whole new light. I can't deny the flutter of excitement that his eyes send whirling through me. But I don't move closer toward him, and he doesn't step closer to me, and the intensity fades to awkwardness.

"Well, I should probably get going," he says, "I've got some errands to run."

"Okay."

Matt has a knowing smirk on his face. "Yeah, maybe I'll get to see *you* later."

I pick up the kitchen towel and snap it toward him. "In your dreams, mister."

"You bet. Every night." Laughing, he grabs his coat and leaves.

I can't help but wonder what this new dynamic means between us. But for now, I'm content to enjoy the playful banter and the warm feeling I'm getting from being around him.

After Sarah wakes up and has breakfast, I set her up to play in the living room with a stern warning to stay in the house. As she entertains herself, I upload the photos I've taken over the past few days to Instagram and Facebook. My friends are going to be sick of all my postings of snow.

A moment later, my cell starts ringing. It's my friend, Terry, a gal pal from back home.

"Wow," she says soon as I pick up the phone. "I think I want to go to Leavenworth next year for my Christmas break. Who the heck is the guy you're staying with? Can you bring me home one of those for the holidays?"

Terry is always able to make me laugh. "I think he's one of a kind," I reply. "And he's nice too."

"*Girl,*" she says in her irrepressible tone of voice. "Any chances of you two hooking up?"

"Terry!" I exclaim. "I have Sarah, remember?"

"Right. Does he like kids?"

"So far, he's been great with her. She adores him." *He'll make a great father someday*, I think, but don't say aloud. If I did, Terry would *never* let up on me.

Even so, perhaps I'm being too obvious because the next thing Terry says is, "Sounds like husband material."

"I don't think so. And even if he were, I'm only here until my car's repaired. He's made it clear he has no desire to live in the city. So, no. Definitely *not* husband material."

"I think the lady doth protest too much."

Rolling your eyes does no good when the person can't even see you. "We aren't even dating! I'm just a guest in his house."

"Well, maybe he could be a holiday fling?"

Back to square one. "I'm not good at flings. Besides, I want a man I can count on to hang around, and that's difficult—more so because I have a kid."

"Okay, tell me this. Have you thought about sleeping with him? From the photos you've posted of him, he looks pretty hard to resist."

I let out a sigh, and I knew that would be enough for my friend to speculate. So I might as well tell her the truth. "Honestly? Maybe once or twice. But it's *not* going to happen."

"We'll see," Terry teases.

"No, seriously. I'm just here on vacation. We may flirt, but I'm not getting involved with Matt. It would never work out, and I don't want to put Sarah through the disappointment. It's hard enough to watch her now. I know when we leave, she'll miss him. Heck, after Christmas, I doubt we'll ever see him again once we return to Seattle. He has no reason to go to there, and I have no reason to come back to Leavenworth. So, it would be pointless to start a relationship, knowing it would never work out."

Stating it flat-out like that made me feel sad about the truth of the situation. But perhaps that's what I needed—a little truth-telling, considering how much I was thinking about him.

"Well, it sounds like you know what you want, and that's all that's important. Just enjoy your time there and don't worry about the future. You'll be back in the grind of the real world before you know it. But," and Terry put a lot of emphasis on *but*, "if you get the opportunity, I say go for it. Pretty soon, this will be a memory. And would your rather regret a memory of something you *did* or something you *wish* you did?"

Chapter Nine

MATT

"Hey, what's up?" My brother Grady slides back a chair and sits down.

The bar isn't hopping, but it's not exactly surprising, considering the time and the location.

"Thanks for meeting me," I reply. "I needed to get out of the house."

"Humm. Christmas blues?" Grady signals to the bartender to bring him a beer.

"I've got a bit of a dilemma."

"What, did you get a girl pregnant?" Grady jokes.

I roll my eyes. "Hell, no. That's not why I wanted to talk to you."

My brother snorts. "Then what's your problem?"

"I've got a woman and her kid staying with me," I say, taking a sip of my beer.

"Seriously? You? What happened to—'I don't let a woman stay at my place'?" Grady sits back, grinning.

"This is different. She needed a place to stay after she

crashed her car at the pass. The place she rented was a dumpy rip-off, so I offered my guest room," I explain.

The waitress arrives and plunks down a bottle before heading to the next table. Grady takes a swig. "So, how's that working out for you?" he asks, looking amused.

"Well, that's where the problem lies."

Grady points a finger at me. "You're ready to throw her out?"

I shake my head. "Not exactly."

"Well, well. So, she's getting to you."

"Yeah, but she's leaving after Christmas."

Grady's eyebrows go up. "Don't get involved."

"I'm not."

"Does Les know that you have a woman living with you?" Grady takes another swig of his beer.

I look away. "Of course not."

Grady looks halfway between amused and surprised. "You going to tell her?"

"No." I run my hand down my beard.

"Why not?"

I sigh. "I don't know."

"What you mean is you don't *want* to know. You don't want Les wrecking your time with this new gal, I take it."

I pause. Put like that, it sounds sort of calculating. But until I figure out what's going on with Paige, I don't want to mess up the status quo. "I guess so," I finally admit doubtfully.

"Sounds to me like you're more worried about your house guest's feelings than Les's." Grady takes another gulp of beer.

I feel a twinge of guilt, but everything with Les has been spelled out in advance. I don't like surprises—either giving or getting—and so I clearly defined the limits of our relationship ahead of time. "That's probably true."

Grady leans back in his chair. "I know you're trying to do the right thing by taking this gal in, but you need to be careful."

"What do you mean?"

"You're obviously attracted to her. But she's vulnerable right now. She has no place to go. Her Christmas plans were probably ruined, and you come along playing the hero. She's most likely been stroking your ego, too. So, it would be easy to get caught up in the moment and think there's something more to it than there is."

I run my hand down my beard. "I know. But... there's something about her, Grady. I'm not kidding. I'm trying not to take advantage of her or anything. I just want to help her out."

"Okay." Grady holds up his hands. "But if you ask me, you're headed for disaster if you cross that line."

"I don't want to lead her on. She's already been through enough."

"Then don't."

"Thanks." I finish off my drink. "I needed to hear that from someone."

"Anytime, bro." He claps me on the back before we leave.

I walk back to my car and sit in the driver's seat. It's less than a week before Christmas. I cross my fingers, hoping nothing goes wrong—and I can resist temptation—before then.

Chapter Ten

MATT

My cabin has started to feel claustrophobic with all three of us there and my determination to not start something with Paige, and so taking this trip up to deliver Karl's annual Christmas treats is a welcome diversion.

Mom texts me her house is full of kids running around, so rather than leave Paige and Sarah home by themselves, I decide to ask if they'd like to come along while I pick up the package for Karl and take it out to him. They have to be bored at my place with no one to talk to but me, and I'm sure Sarah will enjoy playing with other kids for a change.

I text Mom back to let her know I'm bringing them over so she won't be surprised when my usual solo appearance morphs into a group.

"I do this every year," I answer Paige's question as we're driving to Mom's. "Karl Hutchinson is a recluse who lives off the grid, and I make a trip up the mountains to deliver a few gifts and supplies to him. I hope you don't mind staying at Mom's while I jet up there and back."

"That sounds very thoughtful of you, Matt."

"It's nothing. I enjoy getting the snowmobile out every once in a while."

As we pull up the long driveway to The Big Haus, my mom's bed-and-breakfast, I can see the outside is fully decked out for Christmas. The front porch is illuminated with colorful lights, and wreaths and garlands are hanging from every corner.

Paige rolls down the car window and starts taking pictures with her phone. "Your mother owns this? It looks like a Christmas card. I should've booked reservations here," she beams.

I chuckle. "You mean get on the waiting list. This place books up fast for the holidays."

Sarah's eyes are wide with excitement as she runs up the porch stairs, taking in all the decorations. A large bear in a Santa suit sits in a rocking chair with a Flexible Flyer sled leaning next to it. Several pairs of snowshoes line the deck.

As we walk inside, the first thing that catches my eye is the massive Christmas tree in the corner of the living room. It's a real beauty. Every inch of it is covered in ornaments, tinsel, and lights. I know there are several smaller trees throughout the house, each with unique decorations.

Garlands of greenery and twinkling lights wind up the staircase and banister. From years before, I know wreaths hang on every guest's bedroom door, and beautiful holiday arrangements adorn the tables in the living room. The aroma of apple cider, vanilla, and cinnamon fills the room.

The windows are covered with curtains made of red and green plaid. Holly with red berries drapes down from the wooden mantle above the fireplace. There are even a few sprigs of mistletoe hanging from strings in discrete places.

"This is incredible," Paige says as she takes in the festive atmosphere. "Your mom really goes all out for Christmas."

I smile. "She loves this time of year. It's always been her favorite holiday. She goes for the traditional look, though. You won't find any cucumbers or pizza on her trees." Paige punches me in the shoulder in mock upset, laughing.

Just then, my mother wanders over to greet us. "Matt, it's so good to see you!" She kisses me on the cheek. "And who do we have here?" she asks, her eyes flickering over my guests.

"Mom, this is Paige and Sarah," I introduce them. "Paige is staying with me for a little while."

My mother's eyes sparkle as she looks at Sarah. "Well, hello there, young lady. You are absolutely precious!"

Sarah smiles shyly and asks, "Is this where Santa lives?"

"No," Mom laughs. "But it looks like a place he might come to visit."

I can sense the wheels turning in my mother's mind when she turns her attention back to Paige and the luckless guy standing next to her—me. "And how did you two meet?"

I hesitate for a moment before answering, knowing that my mother is always curious about my love life. After I tell her, my mother chuckles. "Well, isn't that romantic."

Paige looks at me, and I can see the hesitation and uncertainty in her eyes.

Perhaps she senses we need a breather because my mother says, "Sarah, I have some hot chocolate in the kitchen if you're interested."

Sarah's eyes light up, and she nods eagerly. "Yes, please!"

"Paige," says the matchmaker, also known as my meddling mother. "Would you like to accompany her?"

Smart enough to know when she's being dismissed, Paige

nods and heads through the same swinging door her daughter just disappeared through.

My mother turns to me. "I'm glad you're helping out someone in need, Matt, but I'm frankly a little surprised. You've always valued your space."

I want to avoid going into any more detail. I'm afraid of what she—and I—might find out. "Thank you for letting Paige and Sarah stay here while I run to Karl's. I'm sure they're enjoying getting out of my tiny place for a while."

"I've packed everything, including a couple of apple pies. I remember you telling me how much he liked them last year."

"Perfect. I tuned up the snowmobile last time I was here, so it should be in great shape. I'll go change into my clothes. Tell Kim to get her butt in gear so we can be back before dark."

"I'm sorry, son. Kim was planning on going, but she and Cody have been performing a lot of Christmas events, and she's just tuckered out."

Just then, Kim walks into the room, bundled up in her winter gear. "Ready to go, Matt?" she asks.

But my mother seems to have other plans. "Actually, I think Kim should rest. She looks exhausted, and I don't want her to come down with something. I know she has a lot of commitments this time of year, and I would hate for her to have to cancel them. She may not get gigs playing at those parties again next time."

"Mom, I'll be fine," Kim tells her.

"You need a rest. I don't want you going up in the mountains like this. It isn't safe."

On closer examination, I take one look at Kim and have to agree with Mom. She has dark circles under her eyes, although if I tell her that, she'll probably kill me. I don't want to Kim falling off the back of the snowmobile or collapsing at Karl's.

"You'll have to go by yourself this year, I'm afraid."

I'm okay with the idea until Paige speaks up, apparently feeling adventurous. "I can go with Matt, if you don't mind. I've never been on a snowmobile before, and it sounds like fun."

My mother looks at Paige with surprise. "That's very brave of you, dear. But you don't have any winter gear to wear."

Kim, ever the helpful one, has a solution. "Don't worry, Mom. Paige can wear my gear. It should fit her perfectly."

"Will Sarah be okay here until I get back?" Paige asks, biting her lower lip.

"Of course," my mom reassures her. "She'll have a great time. There are other children here for her to play with."

With that settled, I grin at Paige. "Looks like we're going on a snowmobile adventure, then. You ready for this?"

Paige smiles back at me, her eyes beaming with excitement. "Absolutely, Matt. Let's do this."

Chapter Eleven

MATT

At first, I was a bit apprehensive. This is the opposite of staying away from Paige. But now I'm veering towards being excited to share this experience with Paige. I didn't expect her to volunteer to go up the mountain, and I'm grateful to my sister for providing clothes so Paige can stay warm on the trip.

After Paige says goodbye to Sarah, I explain to her what to expect, then help her climb on the back.

The sound echoes through the silence as the snowmobile roars to life. We fly past trees heavy with snow, many with branches bending to the ground under the weight of the white powder. Our fresh tracks carve a path through the winter landscape behind us.

I look back at Paige, who clings tightly to me. She's a trooper for coming along—something I didn't expect from a city gal like her. I wonder if maybe I underestimated her just a little.

As we climb higher, the air grows colder, and the snow deepens. Out in the open area, I do a couple of fancy tricks, not really knowing why I'm showing off for Paige. When I hear her thrilled laughter, my question is answered. I suppose I'd do a lot of things to make her laugh like that.

We head up to a more densely forested area where I have to dodge trees as I cut a path. Perhaps it's the beauty of the winter landscape or the thrill of the ride, but at this moment, I feel like I'm twenty years old again and the world is fresh and new.

Once we pull up to the cabin, I shut off the engine and silence envelopes us once more. Paige climbed off the back. I open the storage and hand her a box. I take the other two, balancing them carefully so I don't drop them as I carry the supplies to the covered porch.

We remove our helmets and stomp the snow off our boots. Then I knock loudly. The cabin is a small, rustic structure that has been there for decades. After a moment, Karl pulls the door open and holds out his arms in an expansive gesture. "Welcome, my boy. Glad you made it. A storm is coming, and I feared you'd have to postpone your trip here." Karl shakes my hand, then pulls me in and pats my back.

I worried about the weather before coming here, but he's been expecting me, so I didn't want to disappoint him by not showing up.

Inside, Paige and I remove our jackets, gloves, and snow bibs, then place them on the pegs in the mudroom next to Karl's winter gear. Even with thermal underwear beneath the jeans we wear, it feels cold standing next to the door.

As we enter the main area of the cabin, I can smell the strong scent of burning wood from the fireplace. The room is dimly lit, with a few candles and lanterns scattered around the small space. Unfortunately, there's no electricity at all.

Karl is wearing a plaid flannel shirt with the sleeves rolled up to reveal his muscular forearms. Faded jeans are held up by black suspenders, and his boots are scuffed and well-worn from the many miles he's hiked through rough terrain. His bushy and unkempt beard hangs down to the middle of his chest. What you can see of his weather-beaten face is etched with lines and wrinkles from a hard life out in the elements. Around his neck, dangling from a leather cord, is the small wooden bear I carved for him years ago.

"This is Paige." I wave at her.

"Well, aren't you a beauty." Karl grins. "I wasn't expecting you to bring me a woman for Christmas, but I'm more than happy to take her." He winks.

Paige's eyes are wide. "She's with me," I reply, hiding my grin with my hand.

"Ah, I should have known. Nice to meet you, Paige." Despite his rough exterior, his eyes twinkle with warmth and kindness that I hope puts Paige at ease.

The room looks pretty much the same as last year. The floor is bare, stained wood, with a few small rugs scattered here and there. A large wood stove is in the corner, radiating heat. Karl also built a stone fireplace that dominates the center of the room, and a pot of stew bubbles away on the metal grate.

We settle down at the small wooden table near the fireplace. The heat from the fire is welcoming, and I can feel it warming my numb fingers and toes. Karl hands us each a mug of steaming liquid. "You won't be thinking about the cold after a few mugs of this." He goes back to check the stew over the fire.

Paige takes a sip, then coughs. "What's in this drink?" she whispers to me once she catches her breath.

I tell her quietly, "Some tea, along with Karl's homemade hooch, I would guess."

Loudly, Karl announces, "I hope you're staying for a meal. I've got a pot on."

I know he's expecting us to stay, and since I'm in no hurry

to leave just yet, I reply, "Sure. I brought along a couple of pies for you that Mom baked."

"You tell your mama, thank you."

As we sip our drinks—more slowly this time, at least in Paige's case—Karl launches into a story about his days of hunting and fishing, entertaining us with tales of close encounters with bears, narrow escapes from raging rivers, and nights spent huddled in makeshift shelters during blizzards. I'm sure he's anxious to talk to someone after spending so much time alone.

The slightly musky aroma of the venison stew Karl is cooking begins to fill the cabin. I wonder how Paige will react to the taste. Being a city girl, I'm guessing she probably never tasted deer meat before and wouldn't like it.

Eventually, Karl breaks off his story to serve us his stew and biscuits. I'm glad to see he included carrots, potatoes, and onions from his stash, as well as bay leaves, thyme, and black pepper, so maybe Paige won't wrinkle up her nose.

I scoop up the stew with chunks of buttery biscuit, savoring each mouthful, while Paige picks out the vegetables and only consumes those. As we eat, Karl tells us more stories of his adventures. Paige leans in closer, and her eyes are shiny with eagerness to hear every detail.

After we finish our pie, I think it's a good time to head out. "We better be getting back now." I glance out the window and start to feel uneasy about the prospect of getting stuck in the snow. The snowstorm is getting worse by the minute. Karl's place is at a higher elevation, which means he gets more snow than in the valley where I live.

Karl, who was watching the snowfall with a contented smile, turns to me. "I don't think you're going anywhere tonight, son. The snow is too deep, and the winds are picking up. You're welcome to stay here until the storm lets up."

"Thank you, Karl. We appreciate it." I glance over at Paige, but can't tell what she's thinking. Her expression seems frozen as she looks out at the storm. "But we didn't bring an overnight bag with us."

Karl claps me on the back. "Don't worry about that. I've got an extra room you can use. It's not much, but it's warm and dry. You'll be comfortable enough, especially since you got a gal to keep you warm."

"Can we just wait for an hour and see if it lets up?" Paige asks, sounding worried.

I glance at Paige. I can tell she's thinking about her daughter. I am, too.

"Are you okay?" I ask softly.

She shakes her head no. "After everything we've been through, I'm concerned about Sarah. She's not used to having me away overnight. What if she's scared? What if she tries to take off again by herself in the snow? It wasn't smart of me to come here at all."

I wrap my arm around her, trying to make her feel better. Tension is rolling off her in waves. "There's nothing we can do about the weather. I know it's hard to be away. But we're lucky enough that Karl offered us a place to stay till the storm's done. I might have been stupid enough to chance it if I were alone, but it's much too dangerous to try and head back now with the two of us. I'll let Mom know we're okay and will be home tomorrow, and you can talk to Sarah yourself."

Paige nods, but the worry is still there in her eyes. I do my best to reassure her that her daughter is in good hands with my mother. Nothing reassures her until we use the phone and call back. While I don't ask to talk to Sarah, I can hear the excited, high-pitched sound of her voice going a mile a minute. After blowing kisses and saying "I love you" about a hundred times before hanging up, Paige's expression seems much lighter. This time, when I say, "She'll be fine," she nods wordlessly in agreement.

The two of us sit down on the log couch, leaning against the feather pillows. Karl stokes the fire, throwing more wood on and fanning it until the flames hop. Then he goes to tidy up his spare room so we can crash there.

When Karl returns, he nods toward my mug and asks if I want some more to drink.

"What the hell. We aren't going anywhere." I hold out my mug.

"What about you, young lady? You look a little wound up."

"I guess so."

"You sure?"

"Sure. Maybe it will help me relax."

I'm surprised that Paige agrees, knowing that she isn't much of a drinker.

As the night wears on, Karl does his best to keep us comfortable and entertained with stories. Finally, he gets up, stretches, and tells us he's going to bed, leaving us on our own.

The fire crackles in the background, and a tranquil mood descends over the cabin. The wind whipping outside sounds like a distant wolf's howl. But inside, I'm feeling warm and in a cozy and intimate bubble as Paige and I huddle under the blanket Karl gave us, talking quietly and trying to pass the time.

"What are some of your favorite things to do?" I ask after a moment. My eyes start out on the fire, but I find my gaze drifting over to her. The light dances and flickers over the features of her face, giving her a mysterious look.

"I don't have time much for myself these days," she replies, darting a quick glance over at me. "I just go to work and come home and take care of Sarah."

I know being a single mom isn't easy. "If you had someone to help with Sarah, what would you do?"

"I'd take a cooking class."

"Cooking?" I smile.

"Is that so hard to believe?" she asks when she catches sight of my smile. "Yes, I enjoy trying out new recipes. I especially like making fresh fruit pies. My favorite is apple."

My mouth waters at the thought of biting into a warm, flakey crust filled with cinnamon and apples, topped with a scoop of ice cream. For a city gal, she sure has a lot of old-fashioned qualities about her. Then I grin. I bet if I follow her on Instagram, I can find photos of the pies she made.

The next question pops out of my mouth before my brain catches up to it. "Do you ever think you'll come back here?" I hold my breath, waiting for her answer.

"Maybe," she says considering the idea. "It all depends on my work schedule and Sarah. I'd like to see what things look like after the snow has melted."

Not *no*. Not yes, of course, but it wasn't no. Things were looking up. "It's beautiful. Have you ever gone hiking?"

"A few times in college. I went with some of my friends. We didn't camp, though. We just hiked up a trail behind a bunch of other people. I was following a crowd."

"On the popular trails close to the city, I take it."

She shrugs. "Yes."

"If you come back in the summer, I could show you some beautiful sights."

I'm suddenly hit with the thought that I may never see her again once she returns to Seattle. I've thought it before, with varying degrees of emotions, but this time, the predominant one is loss. I've been trying to distance myself from her, and then this impromptu trip has turned into something more. I honestly don't know how to handle it—or myself.

And it's even harder to know what to do when Paige snuggles closer to me. It's very natural to put my arm around her, and it feels like every nerve ending comes to life with the feel of her pressed up next to me. I reach around her shoulder and take her hand in mine, running my thumb across the back of it. She fits perfectly in my arms, like she belongs there.

Her cheek is pressed against my chest, and I can feel her take a deep breath before she says, "Thanks for taking us in."

"It's been my pleasure," I reply truthfully. "I couldn't leave you out in the snow."

"The time has been flying by. Soon it will be Christmas and then we'll be going back home."

The truth digs deeper that she's leaving. I want to savor our every minute together before it's too late. So when she turns her head and looks up at me, I lean in, placing my mouth on hers. Her lips are soft and move gently against mine, sending waves of pleasure throughout my body to collect most uncomfortably further south.

I ignore the pleasure/pain of our slow kiss until she pulls back and meets my eyes. I hold my breath, not sure how she'll react next, until a smile spreads across her face. "I guess beards aren't so bad after all."

All of a sudden, I'm kissing her again, slow and deep, savoring the moment. When we break apart again, I kiss the tip of her nose. I need to cool this down.

Instead, more words tumble out of my mouth. "How about…" I take a deep breath, knowing that there are strong reasons for us to stay apart. Good reasons. And yet, for the life of me, I can't remember a single one. "How about we get ready for bed?"

It sounds like an invitation when all I meant was for us to go to sleep. It's getting late. Yet it's hard for me to retract what I said. Her gaze is molten and languid, and she nods her head. I don't know if it's an invitation for what I truly want or a gesture meant to take my words at face value.

When we get to the room, I stare hard at the full-sized bed. I know if we lie down together, it will be impossible not to make love to her. So I say, "Why don't you sleep in here, and I'll sleep in the other room?"

"Are you sure? That furniture we were sitting on didn't strike me as that comfortable."

She's correct—it's just split logs covered in a few pillows. I swallow. "I'll make it work."

"Matt, I've been sleeping with Sarah for days now. I'm sure there's enough room for both of us in the bed."

Torn, I study her face. I want to do the honorable thing. But the prospect of sleeping with her feels impossible to resist. I've been fighting my growing desire for her, but the more time we spend together, the more irresistible I find her. There's no doubt about the chemistry between us. That's not the problem. The thought of being with Paige has always been there since the first night I took her home, lurking in the back of my mind.

The way she laughs at my jokes, the heat in her eyes when she saw me naked in the shower, and the way she touches me casually and not-so-casually—all these things are driving me crazy. I want to take her in my arms, to feel her skin against mine, to lose myself in her. The little voice that carries my guilt at starting something I can't finish is getting fainter and fainter in this small cabin perched up on a mountaintop. Up here, trapped by the storm, there's just her and me, and nothing else seems to matter. The guilt of wanting something I shouldn't is as faint as a ghost. It doesn't seem to matter anymore that she's a city gal, and I'm just a simple man. It's becoming harder and harder to resist her pull.

I swallow hard. Maybe there's some way I can stay strong. Maybe it will be okay. "All right," I finally say.

We lie next to each other, fully clothed, looking up at the ceiling. It's apparent to me that Paige has feelings for me too. I know being alone with her like this is a mistake. I want her, and the more I think about it, the more I realize it's not a temporary thing. I have real feelings for her. Like, long-term, "let's see where this goes" type of feelings. But I'm not sure if she wants me to make love to her or not tonight. This will probably be the only opportunity we have before she leaves, but I'm not going to make the first move. I'll leave that up to her.

At that moment, Paige turns to me. The light is dim, but our eyes lock, and I can feel the tension rising between us. Her closeness is electrifying, and the scent of her is making my head spin. Every cell in my body wants to reach out to her, and my desire is too strong to resist.

Slowly, I reach out and brush a hair away from her face, my fingers grazing her cheek. I lean forward over her and press my lips to hers, softly at first, then with more urgency. Her response is instant, opening her mouth slightly to invite me in and deepen the kiss.

Her hands move up to wrap around my neck. I pull her closer to me, my hands roaming over her body, feeling the curve of her hips, the fullness of her breasts. I can feel my heart racing as my body yearns for her.

As we break apart, gasping for air, my eyes lock onto hers once again. Without telling me with words, I know she wants me, too. I can feel her body trembling, feel her racing heart pounding in her chest.

With trembling hands, I start to undress her. I pull off her top and unfasten her bra, following my hands with my mouth. I feel a current as I run my palms down her soft skin. I tug at her pants and slip them off.

She pulls at my clothes, too. Her fingers slip the buttons apart on my flannel shirt and struggle for a moment with my belt buckle. Her touch makes me shiver with anticipation. In the shadow from the lantern, I lean back and admire her body. She is perfect, and I say so, only to get a soft and delicious laugh from her. I bring my lips to her breasts and she lets out a moan. The last of my inhibitions fall away as I let go of all the apprehensions I've been harboring about making love to her.

In another few moments, I'm making her purr with pleasure as I touch her. I've never been so consumed by desire. I want her to want me so much that there's no longer any doubt in her mind that we belong together. I want to make this moment last us a lifetime.

I sink into her and struggle not to come apart. I slowly thrust, our bodies moving in perfect harmony. The intense pleasure is overwhelming, and her moans fill the air. She calls my name, and our bodies quiver as we surrender ourselves, blending into one.

Afterward, I lie with her in my arms, not wanting these feelings to end. I've never experienced a connection like this before. Maybe we have a chance to make this work. Maybe this isn't just a brief moment in time.

When I wake up in the morning, Paige is sleeping peacefully next to me. A wave of tenderness washes over me, followed by a harsh uncertainty. I tense up. I remember drinking Karl's brew. Then the evening's events began to unfold—and the realization that Paige and I spent the night together, making love.

What am I going to do now? I'm painfully aware that sleeping together complicates things more than they already are. I've crossed a line I didn't expect to cross. Paige told me she hadn't been with anyone since her husband died, so this is a big step for her. But now the responsibility of what happens next is on me.

I manage to untangle myself without waking her up. My eyes dart to the clothing strewn across the floor. I try to be quiet while dressing, so I won't alert Paige. Once back in my "lumberjack" clothes, I slip out of the room.

Karl is sitting at the table in dirty gray thermal underwear. He has a mug of coffee in his hand, and he's grinning like a jack-o-lantern. "Sounded like you two had a nice evening."

I run my fingers through my hair. "Yeah, I guess you heard."

"So, when are you two getting hitched?"

"Oh, it's not like that. We're just friends."

"Mind introducing me to some of your other friends?" Karl winks and laughs.

I'm not laughing. And, at that moment, I look up to see Paige standing there.

I don't know how much she heard or what she was expecting from me after last night. I still can't believe I slept with Paige. No matter how I felt last night—thinking we could make a go of it—I know now in the cold light of day that it was a mistake. That brew of Karl's must have contributed to the situation, because I know it was wrong to fulfill my fantasy of making love to her. Sleeping together didn't solve anything. We live hours away from each other. She's leaving after Christmas, and any future I can picture seems bleak.

Paige was the last person I wanted to hurt, yet I've betrayed her trust. She deserves so much more than one night of passion. But I can't give it to her.

"Good morning," Paige says in a cheerful tone. She walks forward and grabs a mug from the shelf to pour herself a cup of coffee from the pot on the wood-burning stove.

"Morning, sunshine." A mischievous grin fills Karl's face. He pours some booze into his coffee and stirs it. "You want to be *my* girlfriend tonight?"

My brows go up as I throw Karl a look of disapproval. His eyes are glassy. He's probably been drinking since he crawled out of bed this morning.

At Paige's careful avoidance and my harsh glare, he smiles. "Hey, it doesn't hurt to ask. I could use a friend like her."

"Just ignore him," I tell Paige. The guy is just lonely and looking for some excitement in his isolated life. But I'm uncomfortable with the way he's looking at her with hungry eyes.

Paige sips her coffee, not letting on what she's feeling at the moment. But there's no way in hell that last night isn't on her mind. It's certainly at the forefront of mine.

Walking over to the window, I glance out. My snowmobile is covered in a thick layer of white. I turn back to Karl and say, "I've got some work to do before we take off. Got a shovel I can use?"

He disappears for a moment into the back and returns with one, then hands it to me. I slip on my snow gear and my boots. "I'll be back in a bit."

After clearing a path and exposing my snowmobile, I'm cold through and through and need a moment to warm up before we head back.

Inside, I take off my boots and go to the fire, rubbing my

hands back and forth to get the circulation flowing in them again. It takes a moment to realize there's no one else around the communal space. When I look around and don't see Paige, I begin to worry. I shouldn't have left her alone with Karl. He's probably half crazy to begin with, so who knows what he might do?

I quietly enter Karl's dim bedroom, my eyes adjusting to the low light, and pause at what I see. The old man is sitting on the edge of his bed, surrounded by several photographs. As I lean against the doorway and cross my arms, I can hear Karl's gravelly voice as he recounts stories about his beloved wife, Carol, who passed away two decades ago.

Paige proves to be a patient listener, nodding and smiling as Karl speaks, giving him the space to express his emotions. The warmth and kindness she exudes seem to put Karl at ease, and he speaks more freely with her than I've ever seen him do with anyone else. She brings out her phone and scrolls through photos she took of Sarah in my cabin. Karl smiles and tells her what a beautiful daughter she has.

As they continue their conversation, I can't help but admire Paige. I feel like I'm teetering on the edge of a precarious situation. My feelings for this lovely person and, at the same time, frustrating woman have grown. Yet whenever I think about taking the relationship further, all I can think of is all the differences between us.

Being insecure about where the two of us stand is as uncomfortable as wearing too tight of boots. All my doubts flood into my head, leaving me overwhelmed and confused.

It's stopped snowing for the moment, so chances are good we can take off before another round begins. "I think we should go," I interrupt the two of them when there's a lull in the conversation. Karl and Page look up at me, and Karl hurriedly shuffles the photographs together and sticks them in his bedside table. I glance at Paige. "I'll call my mother and let her know when to expect us."

"Thanks, Matt."

"Don't you want to stay for some mush? I can heat some up for ya," Karl says as I punch in my mother's number.

Although he's looking at Paige, I answer as the phone's ringing, "No, I think it's best to go now before the snow starts up again."

After talking to my mom, I head back to the main area. Paige is already in the mud room, pulling on her snow clothes. She's awfully quiet.

"Thanks for coming, Matt. It was nice meeting you, Paige." Karl walks us to the door. Then he grabs Paige, pulls her to him, and kisses her on the cheek.

She looks confused.

"Just a goodbye kiss between friends." He grins.

As we step outside into the cold, the reality of what happened between Paige and me begins eating at me again. I know Paige is processing everything, but I wish she would say something. She's Probably feeling just as remorseful as I am.

"Come on." I lead Paige to the snowmobile. She puts on her helmet and crawls on the back behind me. The engine roars to life, I point the nose downhill for home, and we set off over the fresh snow. The pure, white landscape seems to mirror the mix of emotions I feel inside about Paige and me—the beauty and wonder of our connection contrasted with the cold uncertainty of what lies ahead.

The landscape changes, with the trees thinning out and giving way to wide open spaces. The snow-covered ground stretches out as far as the eye can see, and the only sound is the purr of the snowmobile's engine. After what seems like hours, we arrive back at my mother's place and I shut off the engine.

We both remove our helmets. I realize that something has changed between us. I'm uncomfortable with what I'm about to do next, but decide it's probably for the best. I turn to Paige, not knowing how to approach the subject, but she speaks up first.

"Thanks for everything," she says quietly, not meeting my eyes. Then, "I'm sorry. I really don't know what to say to you about last night. I wish I could go back in time and start over."

Her words strike me in the gut. Even though we're on the same page about realistically accepting that our differences are too big to allow us to be together, my heart still sinks. I nod, unable to find the words to respond, and I berate myself for being a coward and not telling her how I really feel. But I have to face the consequences of my behavior last night, knowing that I'm not what she wants.

As I watch her hurry away inside, my heart is heavy, knowing that I can't have what I want most in the world. Instead, I'll only have the memory of the time we spent together.

Chapter Twelve

PAIGE

The snowmobile flies across the white winter fields. My mind and heart are arguing about last night. I so desperately want to believe this is the beginning of something wonderful, not the end of it. Matt is the most amazing man I've ever met, yet I know he's deeply wounded inside.

Have I made a mistake? Last night, what we shared felt real. But now that we've slept together, he's acting as differently as night and day. Maybe he's just afraid to let me inside. I'm afraid too. Afraid that he will hurt me, and afraid that I'm not strong enough to go through that kind of loss again.

But what if he doesn't really care for me and was only using me for sex? He told me he doesn't want a relationship. What if all he's thinking about right now is how to get away from his morning-after walk of shame?

There are so many unspoken words flying past me, like the snow-covered branches on the trees, that my head is hurting by the time we arrive back at Martha's. It's like I've entered a different world far from the one I shared with Matt before.

Frozen all around me is the love we had, only it's locked away in memory and never to be touched again.

We both take off our helmets and sit quietly for a moment on the snowmobile. He turns to look at me and opens his mouth, but I don't want to let him speak. I don't want him to tell me what he told me before—he doesn't do relationships.

So, instead, I open my big mouth and let the words tumble out. "Thanks for everything," I say and try to keep my voice neutral. But I can't make myself look into his eyes. I'm afraid that if I look at him, I'll tell him I love him. And telling him *that* will be the most painful and humiliating moment of my life because I know he will reject me. Perhaps gently, but it will still be a rejection.

Instead, I tell him what I know he wants to hear. The words that will keep this on a casual footing, like he wants. "I really don't know what to say to you about last night. I wish I could go back in time and start over."

And I do. I want to go back in time to that day we met. When he first held out his hand to help me up out of the snow. When he was still my knight in shining armor and not the man who was going to break my heart.

Matt says nothing, and I have my answer clear as day. He doesn't try to tell me he has feelings for me or that we're making a mistake ending things before they even really begin. So, I climb off the snowmobile and hurry inside before I start crying.

Martha greets me at the door with a friendly smile that almost undoes me. But when Sarah spots me, she comes running over, babbling about all the things she did while I was gone. I drop to my knees and give her a big, comforting hug. Whether the comfort is for her or for me is unclear. But I think we both benefit, and by the time I let go, the tears have receded enough for me to smile.

I can't help but notice that Matt is awfully quiet after I stated my piece outside. Honestly, I'm trying to avoid him, and so I spend less time looking at him and more time interacting with my daughter. It's easy to pretend not to feel someone's eyes on you when you're engaged in admiring handcrafted snowflakes and eating a lumpy cookie that a five-year-old made "all by myself."

However, something isn't quite right. He's normally smiles and sunshine, but now the day is clouded over. Our relationship changed because of last night, and no matter how much I pretend we can return to the same flirty, carefree footing, I know it's not going to be the same. I can feel it in the pit of my stomach.

Out of the corner of my eye, I see him motion to his mother, and they step into the kitchen. I can't hear anything except muffled voices. I try focusing on Sarah, but I'm very curious about what they're talking about.

When Matt returns to the living room a few minutes later, his voice is flat and emotionless as he says, "Mom says that you and Sarah can stay here. A room opened up."

A wave of confusion and hurt washes over me. What is happening? I took the high road and gave him what he said he wanted—I ended things so that we could keep things "casual." Why is Matt suddenly changing his attitude toward me? Even if my heart is involved, I know his is not. But even if he doesn't feel the same way for me, after spending so much time together, I know he must feel the undeniable connection between us. If he wants to label it as something other than love, fine. But it makes no sense that he's being so distant and cold.

"I'll fetch your things and bring them over," he says,

turning to leave without waiting for a response from me.

"What about all our Christmas stuff? Are you going to take down the tree too?" I ask. I realize he's serious, and my anger begins to rise. I guess he takes "casual" to a whole new level. As in, he'll sleep with a woman and then leave her high and dry without so much as a, "Thank you, ma'am."

Matt rakes his fingers through his hair, looking stressed. "Since you'll be here till your car's ready, there's no point in keeping the tree up at my place. I'll bring over your ornaments with the rest of your things."

I glance at his mom for clues, but she just shrugs. As Matt walks out the front door and shuts it behind him, I don't know exactly what went down, but it feels like he wants nothing to do with Sarah and me. I have regrets about sleeping with him, but I know that it's because I can't do casual like he can. I haven't been with anyone since Skip died. Now, I feel vulnerable and taken advantage of—something I never expected from Matt.

And what about Sarah? I glance down at her, and see that she's staring at the door as if waiting for him to come back. I don't mind so much that he might dump me off here (okay, I do mind it—quite a bit, in fact), but how can he do that to my little girl?

Martha comes up to me. "I'm sorry," she frowns, looking at the front door where her son has disappeared. "Matt's ... Well, he told me he thought it would be better for Sarah to celebrate Christmas here instead of at his place."

I turn to Martha, trying to swallow back my pain. "Thank you so much for letting us stay here. I appreciate it," I say, giving her a weak smile.

She pats me on the arm. "Don't worry about it, dear. I'm happy to have you here."

"It looks like we're staying here, kiddo," I say, ruffling Sarah's hair. She starts jumping around with excitement, but I'm having a hard time joining in on her excitement. She doesn't notice that my smile is fake, which is a relief. Fake it till you make it, as the saying goes.

"I can show you to your room now, if you like," Martha offers.

I turn to Martha. "Thank you. I desperately need to take a shower and to get out of Kim's clothes."

Sarah's face lights up. "Can we play a game, Mommy? They have lots of games here."

"Sure thing, sweetie. I'll go check out our room, then freshen up. After that, we'll see what fun activities we can find around here to do."

I follow Martha upstairs while Sarah runs off to join the other kids in the bonus room. Once I'm alone, I burst into tears. Matt's rejection hurts like hell. Sleeping with him was a mistake, and I should have never let my guard down. The only comfort is that he ended up being right about one thing—staying here is the best thing of all for us. I don't think I can bear to be around him if he's only going to give me the cold shoulder.

There's a knock on the door, and I look up to see Martha.

"Here are some clean clothes for you." She hands me a bundle. "These are some of Kim's things that you can wear until Matt brings yours over."

I look at the clothes in my hand and just set them on the bed. My emotions are going haywire. "Thank you," I sniff.

"Are you okay?" Martha lays her hand on my arm.

I bite my lip. "I'm not sure."

She pauses before asking, "Did you and Matt break up?"

I shake my head. "We couldn't break up. We were never

together in the first place."

"So, there was nothing going on between you two?" The look in her eyes is skeptical.

"No... not until last night."

"I'm sorry, dear." She gives me a sympathetic look and puts a comforting hand on my shoulder. "I know what you're experiencing must be painful."

I sigh heavily and nod. I wish I could take it all back, starting with my rejection of Matt outside. I want Matt to come back so we can talk about what happened last night. To tell him that I'm not going to pressure him into anything, but maybe we can spend the rest of my Christmas holiday together. I'd rather take home bittersweet memories rather than just bitter ones. I don't want everything to end like this.

"You'll get through this, and you'll find someone someday. It just may not be my son."

I nod, feeling like a zombie. "Thank you for the clothes, Martha. I'll take a shower and get changed."

"Of course, dear. I'll leave you alone now."

As Martha leaves the room, I wonder if I misread Matt's signals up in the mountains. Was it just the alcohol that made everything feel so special? Now, down in the cold, hard light of day, it seems pretty stupid to think that he might have feelings for me. That he might want to pursue a relationship.

I raise my chin. The tear-stained face that stares back at me in the mirror isn't who I want to be in this moment. My heart might be broken, and it may have been a whirlwind few days that might take months, if not years, to recover from, but it is Christmas and I have a five-year-old downstairs, depending on me to make it magical.

Enough of this pity party. I might hurt like hell, but I can get through this. I know I can.

Chapter Thirteen

MATT

My mind is racing with conflicting emotions. I didn't plan on falling for Paige, but it happened whether I like it or not.

Looking around my living room, I feel an uncomfortable tightness in my throat. Her presence is everywhere, and I can't get her out of my mind. The way she looked in my arms last night took my breath away. The feel of her skin against mine made me feel alive for the first time in years.

But it was wrong for me to sleep with her. I dreamed of her for days, but fulfilling the fantasy crossed the line. My brother, Grady, was right. Having Paige here would end up a disaster if I wasn't careful. And I sure as hell wasn't careful last night.

I glance over and picture Paige in the kitchen, laughing while we eat. How many times had Sarah filled my heart with the kind of joy only a child could do? There is a crayon drawing she made for me taped to the refrigerator.

My heart is ripping apart. But, at the same time, there is no way a relationship between us will work. We're from different worlds. Paige lives in Seattle, and I'm not leaving Leavenworth.

I won't ever be tempted to consider that mistake again. And because I can't expect her to change her life for me, my only choice is to walk away now.

Opening drawers, I throw Paige's clothes in her suitcase. Sarah's stuff goes into a bin. I want all reminders of them gone. This is my house, and I need my space back. To rid it of all memories of them. I pull ornaments from the tree and unstring the lights, trying to undo the past.

But each thing I put away only underscores the fact that I'm miserable.

Setting the bins by the door to take to my mom's, I look around. The Christmas tree that once sparkled is now bare. The room still carries the faint odor of vanilla and sugar. A plate of cookies sits on the counter, and I go over in a sudden fit of emotion and toss the plate across the room, sending cookies flying amidst shards of porcelain. Then collapse on the couch.

My phone rings. When I see it's from Paige, I swipe to ignore the call. I can't deal with her right now. I'm afraid that if I don't let her go, I'll beg her to take me back. To give me a chance. And I can just see this city slicker gal looking down her nose at me and telling me that I'm not worth it.

So, I need to come up with a way to make her hate me. I need her to forget about me so that I can forget about her. She'll never find someone else to give her the love she deserves if I'm holding her back.

I come to a realization, and it's a horrible one. It's exactly what I shouldn't do, even if it means we'll have a clean break. The only way to get her to know it's over would be to show her that *I've* moved on. Show her that it's better if she does the same.

Taking Les to my mother's party might be enough to push

Paige away permanently. It can work—if only for one night, I can put on an act and pretend I care more than I do for Les.

I make a quick call to her. "You want to join me at my mother's Christmas party?"

Her voice is enthusiastic. "I would love to."

By contrast, I can hear the hollowness in my tone as I say, "Great." But Les doesn't seem to notice my lackluster response.

"How about taking me to dinner tonight, and then you can come back to my place afterward?"

I hesitate for a moment, considering the implications of what Les is suggesting. It's what she was offering the other night, and I refused. But maybe it's just what I need to get over Paige.

"Sure, why not?" I reply, trying to sound enthusiastic when all I feel is hollow. "But I've got some stuff to drop off first."

When I arrive back at my mom's house, I can see her through the window, bustling around the kitchen. I take a deep breath, grab the suitcase, and head inside. Christmas decorations greet my eyes, and the smell of cinnamon and pine fills the air.

My mom gives me a big hug and a smile, but I can tell she's worried about me. She's always been able to read me like a book.

"Hey, Mom," I say, walking into the house.

"Are those for Paige and Sarah?" my mom asks, gesturing to the suitcase and the bags in my hand.

"Yeah. Thanks again for taking them in. I just thought it would be better if Paige and her daughter stayed with you." I set the bags down on the floor. "I need some space right now."

"Do you want to talk to her?"

"I can't, Mom. I have a date with Les."

"Leslie Bird? Tom's daughter?" She frowns.

"Yeah." My voice is less than enthusiastic, and her frown deepens.

Like all moms, my mom gets right to the heart of the matter. "Matt, Paige seems like a nice woman, and her daughter is charming. Why are you dumping them here?"

"She was stranded in the snow, and I took her in for a while. This is a much better environment for her to be until her car is ready."

"You think Tom's daughter is a better option for you?"

"Mom, Paige is a tourist and is just passing through. She doesn't live here."

Martha crosses her arms, and I recognize the stubborn jut of her chin. "You could go visit her. Seattle isn't that far."

I sigh. "Mom, it's my business, and I don't want to discuss this. I need to leave."

"You may end up regretting it." Her voice echoes with meaning, and I don't have the energy to engage with what she's saying. I've made my choice, and it's the best choice for both of us. This argument is pointless.

Mainly because I know mom is probably right. But I need to consider Paige and her daughter. Pursuing a relationship with anyone scares the hell out of me, so what kind of father figure could I be to a little girl who already lost one parent?

"Mom, I appreciate your concern, but this is my problem. I don't know if Paige and I are meant to be, but right now, I just need to back away."

I could tell Mom's disappointed in my response, but perhaps not surprised. "Okay, Matt. I won't push this any further. I just want you to be happy. But I think you are making a huge mistake."

Nodding, I look down at the ground, unable to meet her gaze. "I know, Mom. Thanks. I know you care."

I can't stop myself from glancing back at the house when I leave, knowing Paige and Sarah are in there. Paige rejected me, and I mutually rejected her, but I never even said goodbye to Sarah. It breaks my heart. She's probably wondering why I would abandon her.

* * *

As Les and I sit down for dinner, I struggle to maintain a lighthearted conversation. We drink wine, share some laughs, and reminisce about a few good times we've had in the past. But I can't help but compare her to Paige and everything she does—from her laugh to the way she looks at me, to how she tosses her hair over her shoulder.

After dinner, we take a leisurely walk hand in hand along the main street of town while I listen to her jabber on about the house she wants to live in someday and how she plans to decorate it. Somehow, the Christmas lights here tonight don't hold the same magic as they did on the day I brought Paige and Sarah into town. Instead, they feel empty and cold, as if their holiday spirit has drifted away.

After our stroll, I drive Les back to her place. Inside, she's created a comfortable and inviting atmosphere, complete with soothing music, dimmed lights, and a bottle of fine wine. I feel an odd sense of déjà vu, although with an even greater disconnect from before. We sip from our glasses, making ourselves tipsy and dulling my pain.

Les is getting bolder with her teasing, and I know where this is headed. Where it almost headed last time I was here. I hesitate, torn between taking what Les is so obviously offering and the powerful emotions I harbor for Paige.

I tell myself I need to forget Paige and move on. I lean in for a kiss, focusing on the gentle pressure of Les's lips against mine, the faint scent of her perfume, and the sound of our breathing as it synchronizes. I try to immerse myself in the here and now with this beautiful woman who is obviously attracted to me, hoping that this will be the turning point I need to move forward. I kiss her deeper, wanting to let Les take me down the deceptive road of desire.

My phone buzzes, and I quickly let go of Les and reach for it. It's Paige. I let it ring for one second before I reject the call.

I've been trying so hard to forget about Paige, but she keeps coming back to haunt me. Now, all my plans about forgetting are blown out the window. I sit up and run my hands through my hair.

"What's wrong?"

I look over at Les in her state of undress. She's gorgeous and smart. Local and interested in me. Everything I know I should want.

My phone buzzes again, and I blow out a breath in frustration, thinking it's going to be Paige again. When I see the name, I mouth, "My mom" to Les. I stand up and walk a few steps away from the couch before I pick it up.

"Hello?"

"Hi, dear. Is now a bad time?"

I look over at Les sitting on the couch, her clothes disheveled. I turn back to the call. "It's fine."

"Good. Because I want to ask you about the Christmas party. You know we're expecting quite a crowd..."

"Yes?"

"I'm hoping you can come over tomorrow with your plow and clear off that lot at the back. You know the one? The one for overflow parking."

"Yes, I can do that. When?"

"Anytime tomorrow. As you know, the party's not for a couple days."

I glance at Les again. She's now tapping her nails against her arm, her whole body language screaming her impatience.

"I see. Okay, I'll do that."

"Thanks, dear. Goodbye for now."

"Bye." I hang up the phone and turn to Les. "Sorry," I tell her. "My mom wants me to plow for her."

I feel guilty, but it's not *really* a lie. More like a lie of omission. "I have to go."

She raises one penciled-in eyebrow at me, and I can feel the waves of disapproval flowing toward me. "At this hour?"

"There's a time limit," I hedge. "I'll make it up to you, I promise."

Les looks at me skeptically, but she doesn't press the issue. "Okay, drive safe," she says, and I can tell she's disappointed.

I feel a mix of relief and guilt. I know that I can't keep using Les to distract myself from Paige, and that eventually I'll run out of excuses not to sleep with her and have to either put up or shut up. There might not be much more stringing along with Les before the string snaps.

"Sorry. I'll pick you up the night of Mom's party around eight p.m., okay?" I want to get out of there before she starts nailing me with questions that I don't want to lie to.

After she says "yes," I head for the door. Les's eyes are on me. I know she's pissed, but I just can't bring myself to be with her.

Outside, I inhale the fresh air. The snowflakes hit my face like a slap.

I am a pathic disaster.

Chapter Fourteen

MATT

The night of my mother's Christmas party, I pick up Les in my SUV, and I compliment her on the new dress she's wearing. I'm trying to be attentive and listen to her when she tells me about her job. While I drive, I can't help but feel like the biggest asshole in the world. I came up with this plan, but I now feel sick to my stomach. My feet are like lead as I walk up the stairs to join the other guests in my mom's bed and breakfast.

When I catch sight of Paige, I'm taken aback again by how beautiful she looks. I ache from realizing I'm about to hurt her intentionally. My plan is to act like Les is the only woman I'm interested in, which is a complete and total lie, of course. But I want Paige to think I've lost interest in her, so she can lose all interest in me.

I play my part with Les, laughing with her and whispering in her ear. When I look up, there's the moment I planned for and never wanted. The hurt in Paige's eyes tears me apart inside, and I question why I'm going through with this charade when Paige is the one I want to be with tonight, not Les.

When we step into the hall, Les pulls me in for a kiss. I see

Paige out of the corner of my eye, so I play along and deepen the kiss, hoping that this will be the moment Paige needs to walk away.

I glance up, and Paige is nowhere to be found. Perhaps I'm just twisting in the knife, but I excuse myself and go upstairs to look for her. I want to confirm that whatever we had is over and that she's ready to move on.

At the end of the long hallway is the door I'm looking for. I hesitate for a moment outside it, leaning against the doorframe.

I don't want to do this. Instead, I want to wind back the clock to that mountainside where we were caught in a storm and trapped outside of time. I want to spend another magical night with the woman of my dreams, knowing that there is only me and her and no one else matters in that moment except the two of us and what we feel for each other.

Instead, I straighten up my back and shake the tension out of my shoulders, almost as if I'm preparing to go into battle. I raise my hand and knock on the door.

Les and I drive in silence back to her place after the party. I feel an awkward tension between us. She's leaning against the window, gazing out at snow coming down.

Once we reach the door, Les turns to face me. There is no softness in her expression anymore as she asks, "You're planning on coming in, aren't you?"

I look at her, unsure how to respond. I'm spiraling down and don't want to pretend anymore that I have feelings for Les. I know I don't. And, unfortunately, I never will.

"Matt, you didn't answer my question."

"I... ahh."

"Are you coming in or not? Because you owe me."

"Owe you?" My eyebrows go up. "What? Am I your stud service?" As soon as I say that, I immediately regret it.

She glares at me.

"I'm so sorry, Les. I didn't mean that."

I can tell the anger is rising in her. She gives me a shove. "I thought you cared for me, Matt. I even toyed with the idea that we had a future together."

"I told you I wasn't into relationships," I say.

"You didn't act like it tonight, which is why I asked you to stay."

What did I expect? I had given her mixed signals. I'd focused on myself, not her.

Les shoots me a glance, her eyes showing her pain and anger. Then she just spins around, walks into her house, and slams the door.

Standing there, I feel numb. I'm on a roll—I successfully managed to lose the trust and respect of *two* women in just one night.

Chapter Fifteen

PAIGE

It's the night of Martha's Christmas party and I have no idea what to expect. Will Matt show up and apologize? Will I?

Soon, the guests began trickling in through the door in ones and twos. The party is suddenly lively, everyone laughing, lights twinkling, and the warm, savory food smells amazing. Sarah disappears upstairs to join the other children, leaving me to mingle with the adult guests.

I'm stunned when Matt comes through the front door, arm-in-arm with the same woman I'd seen him with at the coffee shop in Leavenworth. As they walk toward me, my stomach churns sharply with jealousy. They look so happy together, laughing and whispering to each other, and I feel like such a fool and an outsider at that moment. Matt has his arm on the small of her back, guiding her toward me.

As they approach, I try to maintain my composure. Matt hesitates for a moment before introducing her as Les Bird. It feels like a punch in the gut as I realize that she must be his girl-friend—someone he hadn't even mentioned during our time together. I allowed myself to believe there was a chance for something more between us, but now it's crystal clear that I was misled.

I hurry away, not wanting them to see the tears that threaten to fall. I retreat to a quiet corner of the house, trying to regain my composure and process the reality of the situation. It seems that Matt never intended to pursue anything with me, and I'm left feeling foolish and hurt. I guess I was just convenient up on the mountainside and only too eager to throw myself into his arms.

Throughout the evening, I can't help but watch them from the corner of my eye. Les is constantly draped over him, and Matt doesn't seem to object. The jealousy knotting up my stomach is overwhelming, but I try to keep a smile on my face and continue socializing with the other guests.

As the night wears on, I push my feelings aside and enjoy the company, but the image of Matt and Les together haunts me. I can't help but wonder what could have been if things were different. But I know that dwelling on it won't change anything. All I can do is try to move on and focus on what's truly important—the well-being and happiness of my daughter and myself.

Later, I leave to use the bathroom, but as I round a corner in the hallway, I stumble upon Matt and Les sharing an intimate kiss. My heart aches, and I feel a mixture of hurt and sadness well up inside me.

But I'm tired of being sad. My disappointment quickly turns to anger, and I can't help but feel betrayed. I try to keep my composure, but my emotions are getting the best of me. I quickly turn and run upstairs, trying to hide my watering eyes, and retreat to my room.

Soon, there's a knock on my bedroom door. I open it to find Matt standing there.

"What are you doing here?" I snap, my anger boiling over. But then I remember that I need to get a grip on my emotions, and I take a deep breath to find my Zen again. I consciously attempt to regulate my tone, and it works... more or less. "Why aren't you downstairs with your girlfriend?"

"I just..." He runs his hands through his hair, searching for words. "Paige, I'm sorry. I didn't know how to tell you about Les."

"Okay." I grit my teeth, but my voice at least comes out sounding a bit neutral. I drop my eyes to the ground so I won't glare him, feeling a fresh wave of anger coursing through my veins. Again, I repeat the question, "Why aren't you with her, then?"

"I'm sorry. I should have been more upfront with you." Matt avoids eye contact and fiddles with the cuff of his shirt. Lumberjack chic again.

His clothing choice almost makes me smile. Until I remember that some other woman will be taking that shirt off him tonight, not me and my stomach knots at the thought. "We had a one-night stand. A fling," I say, throwing in a deliberate shrug. "You don't owe me anything. In fact, I owe *you* quite a bit."

His head pops up, and he looks at me. His cheeks redden. "You don't owe me anything."

"Oh, but I do!" Okay, a little over-the-top. I lower my voice, trying to keep my emotions in check. "For saving us from the accident, then driving us to two cabins... giving us a place to stay... and then arranging this place." I wave my hand. "I owe you quite a bit, actually. How much should I write the check for?" I reach for my purse.

Matt shakes his head, "I don't want your money! You owe me nothing. I want nothing from you."

Ouch. That really stung. Mainly because he proved to be so true. "Nothing. Gotcha. Well, I came back to my room because I have several things to do, so if you don't mind?" I hold up my the hand, gesturing for him to go.

"I understand, Paige. I'll leave you alone." Matt's voice is soft, and I can tell he's hurting too.

As he turns to leave, I watch him until the door closes quietly behind him. Now that I'm alone again, I slump down on the bed. I can't help but feel an incredible sense of loss.

* * *

It's been a couple days since Martha's Christmas party and I'm dragging around a heavy sadness as I go through the day. Martha drove me to Leavenworth to pick up my car, so I can leave anytime now. I was lucky they could have it for me sooner than expected. I have the urge to drive back to Seattle today, but don't want to pull Sarah away from the festivities here at Martha's place. I plan to leave in the afternoon of Christmas Day after Sarah opens her gifts.

To the backdrop of holiday tunes and cheerful voices around me, I'm counting the hours before we can go. At least Sarah is having fun. I can tell by the laughter coming from the dining room as she and the other kids play board games. She's a little young for most of the games since she only knows how to read a few words here and there, but she joins in quite enthusiastically with her new favorite: Chutes and Ladders.

I sit in the common area of the bed and breakfast, reminiscing about how I ended up here. This certainly isn't what I expected when I drove up that snowy road. After my husband died, Christmas was a painful reminder of what I didn't have anymore—a family to spend the holidays with. My parents died before Sarah was born, so she never had grandparents doting over her. Every year, I took Sarah, and we flew to Hawaii so I could avoid the heartache.

But this year, Sarah begged me for a "real" Christmas like in the movies. That's how the idea of renting a cabin in Leavenworth came to me. It seemed like an answer to my prayers. However, I had no idea the area was so popular. So, when I got around to book a place, all the regular lodgings were taken. I ended up renting a dive far from the cozy cabin I had imagined, and the rest was history. Thank God Matt rescued us when he did, or we would have been in a much worse situation from the get-go.

I bite my lip as sadness washes over me. What started as ideal turned into more than Matt could handle. I don't know why he never told me he had a girlfriend. Maybe he was as caught up in the Christmas fantasy as I had been. I was naïve to hope there was anything more to our relationship.

I scroll through the photos I took with my phone. So much has happened since we arrived—the Christmas tree, the elk, Sarah getting lost in the cold, Matt. If I hadn't captured everything on my phone, I wouldn't believe they actually happened.

I look up when I hear a jingling noise coming from outside. Sleigh bells are ringing like in the song, and children race to the window. I follow them to see what's happening. A man in a bright red suit is standing outside next to a sleigh stacked with sacks. Sarah's eyes widen and she starts bouncing up and down. Martha informed me that Santa would be making an appearance tonight. I'm eager to capture the moment.

Santa makes his grand entrance to a crowd of giggling kids. As he settles onto a cozy wingback chair, children gather around him. First, he hands out Christmas coloring books to each child. Then, one by one, he invites them to sit on his lap and whisper what they hope to get for Christmas.

Later that night, Martha pulls me aside and quietly tells me that her son Grady played the part of Santa. But there's more.

"Grady told me Sarah requested that he let the two of you move in with Matt."

My heart sinks. This is the reason I never dated. I didn't want Sarah to get attached to someone, only to feel heartbreak when they disappeared. She's too young to understand that just because she likes someone doesn't mean they'll always be in her life.

The night of Christmas eve, after the kids are all tucked into bed, I sneak downstairs and place Sarah's gifts under the tree next to the ones other parents have left for their children.

In the morning, the children squeal as they rip into their gifts. We *ooh* and *ahh* as the kids show us what they received.

I notice Sarah has a pout on her face. I try to cheer her up.

"Why don't you try on your sparkly shoes and fairy outfit?" She shakes her head.

"Don't you want to pretend to be a fairy?"

"Magic doesn't work." She juts out her bottom lip.

After learning what Sarah wished for, I understand her disappointment.

"We're going home today, and you can wear them later," I say, trying to ease her disappointment.

"I don't want to go home." Tears are welling up in her eyes.

"Sweetie, we just came here for Christmas. You know that."

"Where's Matt? He's supposed to be here." Her voice trembles.

I honestly don't know what to tell her. "He had other plans," I say, hoping it will be enough.

"But it's Christmas," she protests.

"I know. But it's time we go back home."

"Are you sure you don't want to stay for Christmas dinner?" Martha asks.

I shake my head, giving her a small smile. "No, I want to get back home. I still have time off until the day after New Year's, and I plan to take Sarah shopping and to the movies."

Martha nods. "I know coming here has been bittersweet for you. But I want you to know I've enjoyed having you and Sarah."

A lump forms in my throat. Coming to Leavenworth was a wonderful experience for Sarah, and that's all that matters.

"Thank you for making Sarah's Christmas magical."

Martha smiles, then gives me a hug. "You're always welcome here. And if you're ever in Leavenworth again, don't hesitate to stop by and say hello."

Chapter Sixteen

MATT

My emotions are in turmoil as I travel the road to my mother's house to say goodbye to Paige and Sarah. I've been avoiding talking to Paige, and now it's too late. Mom called to tell me they're leaving town and heading back to Seattle today. It's Christmas Day, and the snow is coming down, the flakes hitting the windshield like feathers with a soft pitter-patter. Trees lining the road are frosted with a fresh layer of snow, their branches bending under the weight. The sky is a deep shade of gray, with no sign of the sun breaking through the thick clouds.

The radio plays Christmas music, and there is a tightness in my chest as I face the reality that they are leaving. The car's heater is cranked up high, but I have a chill that seems to seep into my bones. My mind wanders to memories of Paige and Sarah. Their smiles, their laughter, their presence. I'm filled with regret and sadness over the impending departure of two people who have become such a significant part of my life. I know that I'll carry the memories of Paige and Sarah with me always, even as I move forward without them.

The snow continues to fall, and I worry about Paige driving over the pass in this weather. She doesn't have the skill to navigate the slick roads. The snow continues to fall, covering the ground in a pristine blanket of white.

As I pull up to my mother's house, I steel myself for the inevitable. I see them loading up Sarah's car with plastic bins. I have to act fast. Stepping out of my car, I approach them slowly, my heart racing with anticipation.

"Paige, Sarah, wait," I call out to them, then race over. As I draw closer, I see the sadness in Paige's expression. This is going to be one of the hardest goodbyes I've ever had to say. But I put on a brave face. "I know it's late, but I brought you these," I say, holding out the gifts.

Paige's eyebrows raise in surprise as I hand her the presents. "This one is for Sarah," I tell her, pointing to the one in shiny green paper.

Sarah grins, then tears off the paper. "Look, Mommy, it's a deer. Matt made me a deer." She holds it out for Paige to see.

"That was nice of you, Matt." Paige gives me a half smile.

"Aren't you going to open yours?"

She hesitates, fingering the paper it's wrapped in. "I didn't think I'd see you again."

I sigh. "I know."

Paige looks at the gift in her hands, then holds it out to me. "I can't accept this."

"*Please*," I say.

Perhaps it's the "please" that makes the difference. Either way, I watch as she removes the paper and opens the box. Her eyes widen.

"It's a snowflake," I explain.

"Matt, it's beautiful."

"I wanted to give you something to remember your stay here." My throat is tightening up.

She puts the box in her purse. "Thank you," she whispers.

I can see her eyes filling, but she's trying to pretend she's not on the verge of tears. I respect her boundaries and say nothing.

"Well, we better take off now," Paige sniffs.

"I just wanted to say goodbye before you left." I feel awkward.

"Bye, Matt." Sarah hugs me, and a wave of emotion washes over me as I hold her close.

"I'm going to miss you, kiddo." My voice cracks. I can't believe this is it. I'll probably never see either one of them again.

"Thanks for everything, Matt." Paige leans over, and I wrap my arms around her. God, I don't want to let her go.

When we drop our arms, I feel a great sense of loss. My insides feel hollow, like a helium balloon.

Paige buckles Sarah in the backseat, then crawls in and drives off. I watch as their car disappears down the road.

As I see the taillights turn the final corner, something clicks in my brain. What the heck am I doing standing here? Les was the only woman who was halfway decent in this town, and she turned out to be completely unsuitable. At least, she was unsuitable for me. And that's because she's not Paige.

I see Paige in my mind's eye—her soft blonde hair, her sharp and intelligent eyes, the soft moan she makes when I kiss her throat. Even just thinking of her makes my heart race. How can I just let her go?

I've made a terrible mistake. I impulsively jump into my car. I don't care if I have to follow them all the way back to Seattle, but I can't let them go. Certainly not like this.

As I drive up the mountain, a curtain of snow begins to fall, and I realize this road hasn't been plowed recently. Flakes start coming down pretty quickly, and my anxiety goes up. I see Paige's car weaving back and forth on the icy road ahead of me.

Watching as if in slow motion, I see Paige's car spin in circles, heading for the cliff on the side of road. I panic.

But it slides and bounces off the embankment does another turn then slams into a snowbank against the side of the mountain.

I maneuver to a stop, jump out, and race to her car. I push the snow away from the door with my bare hands and rap on the window. The door slowly opens.

"Are you okay?" My heart is pounding rapidly in my chest. She nods.

I pull her out of the car and into my arms.

As we stand there in the snow, I look into her eyes and realize that I can't do this. I can't keep my feelings hidden any longer. Especially after seeing the woman I've fallen love with almost careen off the side of the mountain.

"Paige." My voice is trembling. "I don't want you to leave me."

Even though I'm holding her—and even though her arms are wrapped around me—she mumbles against my chest, "I have no reason to stay. I have a job in Seattle and you have a girlfriend here."

I lift her chin and stare at her. "Les is not my girlfriend. We've only dated a handful of times. I'm ashamed of my making you think I cared for her when I didn't. It was all an act. I wanted you to believe I was with her to push you away. I could tell you had feelings for me. I was hoping it would be easier for you to move on if you saw me with someone else. I'm sorry I hurt you. I was afraid to take our relationship any further."

At that, her eyebrows go up and glares at me. "Afraid? Don't you think I was afraid too? I have Sarah I need to think about. I don't want her getting her hopes up only to be disappointed when she finds out that the man I'm with is only temporary. I should have never stayed with you in the first place."

"You didn't have a choice."

"If I tried hard enough I could have figure something out."

"I'm glad you didn't. I've loved every moment you and Sarah spent with me. You showed me what I was missing in my life. And I was an idiot for believing there's no hope for us. Please forgive me. Paige I don't want you to disappear down that road and never see you again. I'm willing to do whatever it takes to make this work. I'll drive to Seattle every weekend if need be. I just don't want to lose you."

Paige stares at me. "Matt," she says softly. "I care for you too. But I need to know that you're serious about this. I can't risk hurting Sarah." She shakes her head. "Not again."

"I *am* serious. I've never cared for anyone as much as I do for you and Sarah. Please give me a chance to prove it to you. We can figure out a way to make this work. We just need to try. Please."

The smile on Paige's face starts slowly, but before I know it, those dimples that I love so much have made an appearance to make my heart soar. I don't care who sees us—I kiss her.

When we come up for air, the first thing that Paige says is, "I can't believe I crashed into a snowbank again." She laughs, then heaves a big sigh.

"It must be fate."

She smiles. "This is the second time you rescued me." She gives me a quick kiss on the lips.

I smile. "No," I disagree. "I think you rescued me for Christmas."

We stay there for several long moments, hugging in the snow.

"Are we going back to Matt's house?" Sarah pokes her head out the door at us.

Paige laughs. "For the time being. It looks like I'm going to need my car towed back to Leavenworth."

With my car loaded up, we turn my SUV around. As we drive, I know that things won't be easy. But I also know that I'm willing to fight for our relationship and do whatever it takes to make things work.

And with Paige and Sarah by my side, I know that anything is possible.

Epilogue

PAIGE

"He wants you to go over to the mistletoe so he can kiss you, Mommy."

I blush. "Okay."

My heart races as I move to join Matt under the mistletoe.

As we stand there, surrounded by the soft glow of the Christmas lights, Matt leans in and presses his lips to mine. At first, his kiss is soft and hesitant, but it quickly deepens into something more passionate.

My head spins as I feel Matt's strong arms wrap around me, pulling me closer to him. I can feel the heat of his body against mine, and it sends shivers down my spine.

Everything else fades away, and all that exists is the two of us in that moment. I don't want it to end, but eventually, we pull away, breathing heavily.

"Wow," Matt whispers, his eyes locked on mine. "I'm so glad you decided to give us a chance."

I can't speak, so I simply nod, my heart still racing from the intensity of the kiss.

Matt lifts my chin and I look into his eyes. "I want to make you happy." His voice low and sincere. "I'll do my best to never let you down."

I take a deep breath, my mind dancing with joy. Without hesitation, I lean in and kiss him once more. This is exactly where I want to be—in Leavenworth with him.

* * *

The large dining room is filled with the sounds of laughter and conversation as Matt's family and friends gather around the table. It's elegantly set with candles, flowers, and silverware, making it look like a scene from a movie.

Grady sits at the head of the table, with his mother on his right and Matt on his left. The other siblings and their partners fill out the rest of the place settings, all chatting and joking around.

The food is plentiful, with plates of roasted turkey, mashed potatoes, stuffing, and various vegetables passed around the table. Matt's mother had gone all out, preparing a feast fit for a king.

As they eat, the conversation flows easily, with everyone sharing stories and jokes. I find myself relaxing, enjoying the company of Matt's family and friends.

At one point, Matt's brother brings up a funny story from their childhood, and everyone erupts into laughter.

I look over at Matt, who is grinning from ear to ear. I'm happy to see him surrounded by people who love him. I know he's offered to come to Seattle on the weekends, but I have no desire to take him away from his life here. Leavenworth is where he belongs. I know my skills are in demand and that I can find a job where I can work remotely if my company won't let me. I don't have to live in the city. It's only two hours away, and if I want to shop or take Sarah to the museum, I can stay at a hotel.

As the night wears on, Matt's mother, Martha, shares stories about Matt's siblings. I find myself enjoying the banter and laughter, and I'm looking forward to getting to know his brothers and sisters.

"Merry Christmas."

Everyone raises their glasses, including Sarah. I feel a surge of happiness. It's a gift I can't capture on my phone but can hold close to my heart. I'm looking forward to spending time in Leavenworth with Matt and his wonderful family.

* * *

For other books in the Love in Leavenworth series go to: www. judy-leslie.com

JUDY LESLIE

* * *

About the Author

Judy's been accused of having an overactive imagination since she was a child. So it only made sense that she jot down her stories and turn them into books.

She lives in the Pacific Northwest and splits her time between living in a city on the water and a cabin in the mountains of Leavenworth, Washington.

In addition to writing contemporary small town romances Judy writes mystery romances that have strong emotional elements found in woman's fiction. Her Cook's Cove series contains a little bit of heat along with some darker themes.

For more information about Judy's books go to her website at www.judy-leslie.com

Acknowledgments

I would like to thank my husband and friends for their support. Especially the ladies in my book club for not getting upset with me when I haven't read the month's book. A special thanks goes to the editors that have helped make my stories better and my cover designer for her wonderful designs.

My house hasn't been as tidy and my meals haven't been fancy while I've been sitting at my computer dreaming up stories. But my family understands in order to create it takes time. I am thankful for everyone's understanding.

Love you all!

Judy